where mayflies live forever

where mayflies live forever

anupama mohan

PICADOR INDIA

First published 2022 by Picador India
an imprint of Pan Macmillan Publishing India Private Limited
707 Kailash Building
26 K. G. Marg, New Delhi 110001
www.panmacmillan.co.in

Pan Macmillan, The Smithson, 6 Briset Street, Farringdon, London EC1M 5NR
Associated companies throughout the world
www.panmacmillan.com

ISBN 978-93-90742-53-0

This is a work of fiction. Names, characters, businesses, organizations, places, events, and incidents either are the product of the author's imagination or are used fictitiously. Any resemblance to actual persons, living or dead, events, or locales is entirely coincidental.

1 3 5 7 9 8 6 4 2

Typeset in Garamond Premier Pro by R. Ajith Kumar, New Delhi
Printed and bound in India by Replika Press Pvt. Ltd.

Like the ocean
be vast and unknown,
but if you cannot,
like the river,
be free and forever flowing,
but if that too be hard,
then, still as that mystic water,
be whose deeps no eye can see.

1

WHAT CAN I SAY THAT MIGHT EVEN SCRATCH THE surface of who she was? She was a quiet one, always. When she was born, her face and body had so much hair, I was shocked. As a child, I used to have long, beautiful hair, until the water in Veni's father's house ruined everything. My first thought when I saw her was concern for all that hair. I could sweetly imagine braiding it with flowers, tying it in ribbons, oiling it and teaching the girl how to care for it. After all, when it comes to women, caring for one's hair is a form of self-love. I knew I'd teach all of this to my daughter. Her father, though, had other ideas. He wanted to name her Rajalakshmi. I told him straight – I didn't like the name. I wanted a name that wasn't tied to one single meaning or even to him or his family. He was a sly one – I could see that by choosing the name Rajalakshmi, he was also immortalizing his mother whose name was Lakshmi. That witch! *Ayyo*, for as long as she was able to move about, she was such a pain for me. Now that she is bedridden and cannot walk around due to the stroke, her incessant nagging has reduced, and I no longer have to suffer her criticisms of thisthatandother. So, I put my foot down for 'Sriveni' – she is named after a river, braided hair, a flood; so many meanings the word has.

Like a river in spate,
bearing water like a mother
bears her unborn,
so she goes, in this unseasonal rain
bursting the banks
walk along, if you must,
but step away to let her pass,
walk along, only walk along.

She was my first, and I was beside myself with fear that I might drop her or hold her too tight or smother her when she fed from my breast. I would often give her tiny pinches to make sure she was breathing because when I was a child myself, my beloved pet, a rabbit, suddenly stopped breathing one day and I, who was sleeping next to him, had no idea how long he lay dead beside me under the folds of my *davani*. When I became a mother for the first time, I was so afraid my baby would die for no apparent reason that I watched her all the time and touched her excessively, until the old woman calmed my fears and showed me that she was no rabbit; she was, in fact, a small tornado, a force of nature, and my qualms were put to rest. She was born to be called Veni. Her hair had unmatched beauty and we taught her how to take care of it as one would a sunrise-dream or a precious pearl. That is why I cannot believe she would do what they are saying she did. It is impossible. I shudder to think that Veni would do something so hideous. You see, a mother knows. Would you both like some water? We still keep ours medicated with herbs the old woman taught us about – thc tastc is something else altogether. There you go. What were you saying? Yes, I was saying that in my bones, I can feel it. She will return, my Veni, in all her crowning glory and then you can take your scurrilous chat about her cutting her hair, burning it – my lord! Strike the thought down! You will see what I say come true and then you will be served right, all of you. I don't know why her Appa thinks like the others too. One's own daughter – does one ever abandon one's child this way? Her brothers, the woe that has befallen them. To lose their sister, to have all of life's possibilities cut off, to never be able to dream of ... this is fated to be. But they are loving boys, who, like us, have learned to wait. So long as they remember what Veni is capable of, they know she will return. Don't you remember, *ei* Appayi, that time when she was returning from Pudukottai and the bus overturned? Sixteen children died and so many were injured. Veni's foot was damaged permanently and her dream of being a dancer died right then. We had all thought this would be the end of her dream but when she recovered in eight months, Veni was back to learning at school; it was as if she could not wait to get back into the world. Such a child, you are all saying, has done these things? Is it even possible? But who am I talking to? The old woman barely pays attention to what goes about her. And you people, what have you brought my family besides more grief, more pain? I feel like I'm speaking to walls, but a mother's heart is never wrong; you wait and see. How much love I taught her for her hair, you ask her when you find her. It was the colour of Krishna's face – there was a shine to it even when we did not oil or tend to it regularly. Even as a ten-year-old, she had hair that reached her tiny hips, weighing down her head so heavily that she would cry that her neck hurt. Aatha and I would then sit her down and gently trim the ends while massaging her neck with heated *velakkennai* in which Aatha added some *nilagiri* leaves, castor oil and eucalyptus, an age-old combination in our home for dealing with aches and pains. Then, while the little one was on our laps, we would both take some *ellennai* concoction made by Aatha and I would start by rubbing it on top of the head, the *uccantalai*, and a little behind me, Aatha would take in her hands the ends of Veni's long hair, the fragrance of the sesame oil filling up our little room. She lay there between our laps, her big black eyes looking at the ceiling, playing with her little hands and asking an endless series of questions, and Aatha would tell her of the different uses that household fruits and vegetables could be put to or how one could read the skies for rain or how to do arithmetic in the head with the help of red seeds. Mostly, I would stay quiet listening to the two twitter away, my head filled with other worries but becalmed by the ritual of oiling that I enjoyed privately in that hour of the day. Their chatter left me a rare moment of quiet in that always-busy house, and being silent was a relief. My fingers and palms would heat up as I rubbed and massaged her scalp, making sure the oil penetrated the roots, its nutritive life feeding her hair with health and beauty. Sometimes, I would sing her old songs I had heard my mother and aunts sing. Sometimes, she would lisp along in her child-like way, missing many words and making up her own, and soon, Aatha would be humming too.

> *The noon-sun slipped in through my window,*
> *Its shadows dance on my little one's face.*
> *I catch a dot in my palm, but it escapes!*
> *I almost had it, but you cannot catch the light —*
> *so, I rubbed it on my little one's cheeks,*
> *poured it into her closed eyes,*
> *and warmed her neck with some,*
> *but light comes with her sister, darkness,*
> *and when I played with the shadows,*
> *kneading and cupping the white, alas,*
> *my little one swallowed the black!*

Aatha's oil-making skills were legendary in those days: there was nothing that couldn't go into the oil and provide some rich benefit to the user. Hibiscus was her favourite – *cemparutti* leaves, flowers, fruit, even bark she would add to sesame or coconut oil, along with *kariveppilai, cukku, vendayam, thippili, vēppela, malli ilai, tulasi, vetiver, nellikka* and, of course, nilagiri for keeping lice and other pests at bay. The fragrant mixture could both cool the hair and warm the scalp, and was guaranteed to bring sound sleep, energize the body and calm anger and despair,

Aatha said. But there is no safeguard against sorrow – here, even the old woman couldn't save Veni with her oils or her stories. The house has become soundless now that the expectant mothers don't come any more. At one point, there was no time during the day for any work other than *sewa* to these girls. How that old woman knew, don't ask me. I tried often to learn from watching her, listening to what she would whisper on the swollen bellies of the women, putting my ears to hear what the little *pāpa* said from inside – but no, I didn't have the gift. I heard nothing, could say nothing, and had nothing to contribute other than being an assistant doing Aatha's bidding and carrying out her commands. Still, watching the women come in with their brows all knotted up and leave with big, beaming smiles made my heart sing. And so many brought things to eat: homemade *murukku, ulundhu kali, paniyaram, kuzhambu, laddu, seedai*, whatnot. It was a tribute to the old woman whose hands and words wrought miracles, they said. Aatha's massage skills were legendary: all she needed was some warm oil and the babies blossomed under her deft kneading and pulling. How many babies came into our home malnourished, unable to gain weight, sometimes born prematurely, but Aatha had a practised therapy for each and, under her supervision, the new mothers, so frantic for their tiny darlings, would learn how to hold a tot, how much pressure to put on the baby's tender skin, how to gently exercise the baby by raising its toes to its forehead, releasing gas and helping its digestion. Most of all, Aatha taught that as the largest organ in the human body, the skin was also the most sensitive and human beings craved touch more than anything. Massage was, according to her, a way for love to take the physical form of affection, for, she said, babies who are starved of physical affection grow up warped and stunted in their minds. She held massage to be an indispensable skill for a young mother. How vivid those days stay in my mind – the old woman freely shared the tricks she knew but she kept her best and deepest truths for Veni. She was a teacher worth her weight in gold, I must say, and my own children, all three, thrived under the shade of her care. And why only my children? All the young mothers who came to our home learned how to take care of themselves during and after the pregnancy, for Aatha taught them to be self-reliant and educated the accompanying relatives to look for signs of distress. Aatha's *siddha* made our lives meaningful. You want more of that water? I told you, the taste is not something you will forget. Veni too had it in her, you know, the siddha – she had it though she was but a little one herself. I could see it when she would get the ice water or wet towel herself, her mind independently knowing what Aatha would ask of her. She was so good at grinding medicinal leaves and somehow knew, on her own, how much of the nilagiri was needed, or how to pluck the *venthayam* correctly and how to separate the *lavangam*. The old woman would say mysteriously, Veni has the *siddhi* and then, like the witch she is, she would look at me and quip, your life has some meaning because of this one, otherwise you are one *muttaciriki*! Being called a brainless idiot is all I was good for and her constant badgering used to make me so angry in those days. But in my own way, I taught my Veni things: on nights blacker than the ravine facing the *kovil*'s rocks, when my little ones feared the dark, I would sing to them lines from our ancient poets. And when they were afraid of thunder and lightning, I would tell them of the sweet rain that would come after all this fury. In other homes, children learn to say *Arjunan, Phalgunan, Parthan, Kiriti* but I taught my Veni and her brothers a different chant, one that I made up from the five *thinai* of our ancient poems: *kuṟiñci, mullai, marutam, neital, palai*; the landscapes conjuring up whole worlds for the children lisping the mnemonic. It was sweeter than any lullaby, calming them to sleep on fitful nights. Now the old lines ring so hollow:

All towns are ours. Everyone is our kin.
Evil and goodness do not come to us
because they are given by others.
Nor do suffering and the end of suffering.
Death is not new. We do not rejoice
when living is sweet. When we suffer
we do not say that living is miserable.

But we do! I do! I say now that living *is* miserable, my children gone, even the ones in front of me are lost in some world where my songs of lament do not reach their ears. And I miss the old woman's raspy voice but, most of all, I miss my Veni's face and placid smile – she who could still harsh winds, be like cool water on hot days. Where has she gone leaving us two old women by the cot? How were we to know what would befall this family? Aatha is shrivelling up by the day and has this relentless thirst that will not go, no matter how much water we give her. I am at my wits' end, because I have tried everything, but every ten minutes, she wants to drink and now only spoonfuls are possible. Her voice, however, is still radiant, and when she speaks, she can go on and on until fatigue brings on sleep. I listen when the old woman speaks and imagine our Veni is still here, near. I miss those days when the house was full of noise and people; all of that is gone now.

Our people have scattered; homes have emptied as men and women have gone away to other cities – maybe this is a natural part of life. But we are stuck here – I cannot leave my sons and now my daughter has gone missing. And how will we move when the old woman lies this way? See. She urinates continuously, dripping from the centre of the cot. Appa has put a steel pan under the bed and I keep throwing out the waste every two hours. And yet she craves water, afflicted by a thirst that is beyond my ability to quench. And what to say of our home?

The house is cold at night;
my sons sit, bereft,
their lives grist to fate's ambush.
My daughter has taken her songs
and gone.
I am a mother, who
in a trice,
lost all her children.

How does the day go for me now, you ask? The men leave in the morning after their silent ablutions and do not return until the sun has entered the trees. The boys come for their lunch, which they eat in silence, sometimes not even asking for more until I forcefully put some on their plates. Appa doesn't join for lunch but returns by four o'clock, and then I give him his usual coffee with some fritters, and he waits quietly for dinner. The boys leave home after lunch and return late in the night, having eaten somewhere outside, and while Chinna does what he does, his elder brother keeps guard all the time, both sons lost to me now. And what to say of my husband? When evening becomes night, his fears return, he turns forgetful and is quick to go to sleep, seeking an escape from waking. We talk so little nowadays. And then what do I do? I am turning down the lights, checking with the old woman, as the house grows still as a cemetery. No one watches the television anymore for fear of the news. Veni has taken the sounds of our home with her and tongueless we all are, as we sit, waiting for answers. You might say, I had this coming. I told her to be quiet when it all happened four years ago but I thought like a mother and I wanted to save her from the shame and suffering. You are a woman yourself, Amma, tell me, what would you have advised your daughter? But may God never visit such a fate on you or yours. What am I saying? Women must bear so much in silence and grief: so my mother taught me and so I said to my daughter. Was it wrong, you think? Have the times changed so much for women that there are alternatives? I can't see past this, this fog of shame, so how could I tell my daughter any different? A violation is for all time; like childbirth, we carry its mark for life. Can you rub out the scars? They grow lighter, yes, but they remain. They can, however, be forgotten, little by little, like a bad dream one dimly remembers after many years, only its fear still haunting but all other details slowly misremembered or misplaced somewhere in a pocket of the mind. It can be done. I told her as much, but she wouldn't let it go. She and her husband can work this out, despite the loss of the baby, I told her this. Little *pāpa*, barely knew life. Veni would joke with her brothers she was bringing them a gift but it was so big that wrapping it would take her nine months, at the end of which, she would present them with a surprise. There is no greater sorrow for a mother than the loss of her child, but I say, when you are young, you can rise from even this. I told her and her husband, they could try again for another child, but they needed to leave Sittanavasal. There was too much pain and woe in this place; here, they were like birdlings without a nest, too much in the open, too near the brink of eternal sorrow. But there was also danger, black as sin; nothing is as it used to be. So I suggested to both of them to move to Chennai; I have a few relatives there, and though they all know of the scandal, one or two of them agreed to quietly help. This is what family is for. How many nights I made this plea to this girl, but she would not relent. She had resolved to get back to her school-teaching and couldn't be swayed from that decision. Her husband simply vanished after a point; I don't know if he resigned from his job. I have heard that he has been seen occasionally in hotels, but no one has a fixed address for him. Veni did not run after him which I found so strange and, on this matter too, my pleas went unheeded. A mother is an unwanted thing after a certain age – who will listen to her warnings? Alas, I myself have been guilty of not listening to my mother or Aatha here, but now that it has befallen me, I know what they meant. Someday, Veni will know too. But now, they say, she has gone missing? It is beyond belief what they are saying, that she was seen walking with someone's head in her hand. Is that even possible? Is she some Kali or Durga? She is Veni! Where were these people four years ago when my daughter screamed for help and cried for months on end? My whole family has been shattered by events beyond our control. If there is a god in the heavens, which I now greatly doubt, should my daughter continue to be punished in this way? Has she not gone back to her life the way everyone wanted her to? And what has been our reward? Have you seen my sons? Have we been left alone, and now this? Why have you come with this made-up grotesque tale as if she was some beast hungering for violence? She is a schoolteacher; do you think it is possible for her to do something like this? And to shear off her hair and burn it? Impossible! My fear is that something dire has happened to her and nobody is concerned. No one is looking for her, not in the right places. I told the inspector that her photo should be taken to various towns and used to investigate if someone might have smuggled my daughter there. Who knows how this world thinks? Once a woman is despoiled, she is fair game – maybe some cursed man thought that way. I am terrified that my daughter has been abducted and taken to some hidden place, left without help, at the verge of some tragic outcome. How is my heart to believe otherwise? Is this a world kind to women? Look, I am cleaning Aatha's pot – she who devoted her life to ministering to childbearing women, opened our doors and hearts to needy girls who had no source of support and only unsympathetic husbands who knew no better. Who asked Aatha to do these things? It is a calling, a siddha. My daughter has it too, she always did. And if she is in some place where her life is in peril, with her will perish her siddha too. The world will then truly be orphaned.

2

YOU CAN CALL ME RAJI – IT'S NOT THE NAME I WAS born with but it's the name Veni gave me and it's what I like being called. Ever since I knew Veni she has called me the name her father would have given her, had it not been for her mother opposing it. But it was a name she liked because it tied her to her Appatha and, by giving it to me, Veni was making me a part of her family. She was like that, you know, picking up strays and tending to them until they were strong enough to go their own way. We spent our childhood in such closeness and warmth: her home was a shelter for women who were carrying and I would see her running around helping her Aatha and Amma with the chores, and I would scurry here and there, she leading, nearly a head taller than me, her thick braid hopping wildly as she ran from the well to the kitchen or from the clotheslines to the almirah. Whatever Veni did, I did too, for such was her draw on me that I was always around her as a child, like a sphere orbiting around the red glowing sun. Her little brothers too followed us about, and we basked in the love of mothers and expecting mothers and grandmothers, all that affection, embracing, hand-holding, playing, coddling, kissing, cheek-pulling and storytelling going into our making. How formative were those days – we learned to run to school under the hot sun, forage in the old grounds for mushrooms and wild berries, pick *mullai* for garlanding, my short, coarse hair a far cry from Veni's glorious mane but I was always excited about doing things with her. One of our favourite pastimes is also the source of my most precious memories – it was when Veni and I went picking mullai and *malli* for the women who came to their home. Beating the red ants, we would shake the flowering tree, trying to make the flowers fall down in a torrent and making our work easier. When I close my eyes, I can still remember the breeze, wet soil, and incredible fragrance of the flowers when we brought them in baskets to Veni's home. If dreams had a fragrance, it would forever be the scent of jasmine for me. I called her mother Veni-Amma in deference to everything that belonged to Veni. You could call me Veni-Raji and I would answer to that name. Aatha and Veni-Amma taught us to thread the flowers and how many hours I spent in their home laughing, learning and breathing in their love and joy, so much in excess that they had enough to go around for those of us who came knocking at their doors, longing to be included, to belong. What makes little girls so light and fearless and open-hearted to others, to life? Now it seems like an idyll edged by darkness, two girls in their tinkling glass bangles and anklets, surrounded by untold evil, existing on the lightest of breaths, only a misstep or bus ride or skipped auto away from that giant shadow of malevolence that always hovers around little girls and young women in our lands. What terrors we live ignorant of and we call on gods – Muruga, Ayyappa, Karthikeya – to protect us and we call on goddesses – Mariamma, Meenakshi, Pēchithayi – when our wounds burn in the sun and do not cool at night. No god or goddess comes to my mouth now; I have thrown them aside because they are no good to me anymore. I came from nowhere and now I know there is nowhere to go but on this one earth, where we meet life and we meet death and in between ... what is in between? But you are not here for my idle chitchat; you want to know who I am and how I know Veni, right? They say my mother was called Savithri and my father was a Muslim fisherman but all I have known my entire life is that I'm an orphan and if it were not for my mother's sister, I would have been far,

far away in an orphanage or in someone's kitchen washing their utensils and cleaning their homes. But as it happened, Sittanavasal was destined to become my home and Veni my heartbeat. Where has she gone, you have come to ask? Ask instead: why is she missing? How many of us must go missing before you all notice? And if you think you will get anything from me, you are mistaken. What are they saying in the marketplace? I heard that his headless body was trembling on the ground like it had been hit by an electric current and blood poured out of his severed jugular – can you confirm? Is that true? I hope to God it was true! I wonder how long he felt the pain ... or was it all over soon, all too soon? Hah! You both look at each other because you think I am speaking like a mad *bhadrakali*, no? *Bah!* She did it, you think, right? Why did she do it? Is she coming back? These you want to know the answers to, eh? These are the wrong questions, but you have come to the right place, for I will show you how to ask the right questions. That's right, get that pen dancing on that notepad. Write. Question One: do you know what it feels like to have your vagina split open? Many women suffer from it at the time of childbirth as the canal widens for the child's body to come through. But do you know what it feels like to go through repeated and unrelenting intercourse? With fingers and whole fists and penises? Well, until you know the pain of splitting from your seams, do not come back to me to ask stupid questions. And when you know that pain, that eye-exploding, heart-stopping, stomach-burning pain, then you go sit in a tub of warm medicated water for hours, hours until out of exhaustion agony and madness, you sleep. You sleep sitting there like a great blessed sage, because your body is not yours, only the pain is and the scorching humiliation branding through your face into your throat and down your breasts and into the stomach and all the way to your vagina where it roars into a fire and torches the vanishing pain once again like a bellow on an anvil, jerking you awake just as you thought death was coming in your sleep and you could, just could be so lucky as to step across all that pain into blessed sleep. Your face twists with my words, no? So, let's move to Question Two: can you imagine – do you know this word *imagine* – if you do, you lucky bastards, you will survive this because all you have to do is imagine while my sister, my heart's beat, lived through months and months and years of pain until no recovery was possible; only a stony cave inside her vagina all the way to her empty womb where dead weeds grew instead of life and forever closed down her body, the only temple a living being has to call its own, a line that separates you from me, that line breached forever, only fragments left once four men had done what they wanted with her body and left her to die. When you know this, when you can imagine this, you come back to my home and I will swallow my spit and taste its burning acid instead of wasting it on you. What is it that you drink? Is it water? You know when we first gave her water her face twisted in pain and nearly choked as if we had fed her shards of glass. Can you imagine that your mouth is turned inside out and no matter what you drink how much you drink there is only this undying poison inside so acrid that your tongue shreds each time you open your mouth and the very air raises blood which you keep down because you cannot spit nor hold, you cannot open nor close? Now, with your mouths gone, use your eyes: think of what you like in a woman. Question Three: is it her hair? Gorgeous, sensuous, the mark of her femininity, a blessing from God himself – seduced as even he was by the beauty he made and gave to woman, daughter, beguiled over and over until a woman's hair becomes the noose by which she asphyxiates, just as they tried with Veni, laughing that corrosive raucous laugh that tore into her flesh, their contempt lacerating her skin in a thousand cuts from which they sought to leach her of her life force. Her hair they grabbed by the fistfuls, spitting vile names at her fierce tresses so beloved of her Amma and Aatha. She remembers, she remembers all of it and wears her hair now, unmindful of its beauty, dismissive of its purity, needing none of it – you say she burned her hair? *Burned* all that beauty off? *Shabaash*, I say! Go look for her hair, pick up every discarded strand and build a temple for each and ask, pray, *beg* to be healed. And when your scoring mouths and gangrenous moral order heal, you ask what is the first morsel of food you want to taste? Is it something salty? Is it something sweet? Or do you prefer that old penchant for spicy that now seems like a memory writ on water, the dimmest of memories because a life without justice is a life cursed to eating ash and stuffing your mouth with cotton drenched in the last great smell you remember – maybe the musk of a penis in heat or the garlic of an unwashed cavity a man calls his mouth or the offscourings of *sambar* crusted into the nails of your violator who forces his hand down your vagina and brings his fingers back to plough your nose, all in jest of course. Then you can *imagine* that every time Veni took a morsel to her mouth, she gagged because the smells of her attackers came to life and food itself became a curse to be lived over and over and over again. You know food? – your amma's best curry or your wife's most delicious sauce or, hey, you're lucky, no? You bastard? You're lucky so your daughter made her charming, unforgettably aromatic *mor-kuzhambu* because she, *chinna pāpa,* made it for her dear appa, no? That food, that food becomes bile and faeces and sewage in your mouth day after day, month after month, until you decide food need not taste, it can simply go down your throat to your belly and become the sewage it always was and that black waste nourishes your empty cave of a body and you are that big gaping hole the men enjoyed and threw things into – that abyss they yelled abuses into until the sounds echoed through her insides and pounded her ears and eyes. Since the sounds had nowhere else to go, they merged into her flesh, became her very tissue and muscle and bone, and she was that body they had torn apart, that body they had left behind, that body you have come to question me about. So, you bastards, you take your questions and stuff them in your backside and you come back when the blood from your eyes and ears and the hollow echoes inside your heads make it unbearable to not know where Veni is, to not know what she had in her hand as she walked, to not endure the mystery of her death and her life. You come back then and Raji might speak to you but, mind you, you bring a bomb along that you can fling or an *aruval* at least because my mouth will clench and I will not speak, so you will have to prise my face open and, with blood, paint my mouth back on my face where my smile used to be and I will still not say a word to you and your newspapers, courts, lawyers; you will not get a word out of Raji because I am already with Veni, wherever she is and I am holding what she held in her hand and I am dancing and I am howling because where she took one, I would have taken four, cutting out two more arms for myself to hold four heads, where she, in all kindness, in unbearable mercy, took only one. So, take your jeeps and your guns and you go to the four who remain and you tell them to become really, really small, so small that they are nearly invisible; tell them to live every single waking moment of their life caressing their heads, touching their skin, kissing their babies and fucking their wives happy with doors and windows closed and not a crack open to let the light in because until my last breath I will walk this world with a sickle in my hand and a revolution in my heart.

3

THERE WAS A CUT ON HER THIRD TOE THAT BLED lightly. It must have been the rocks she had to navigate as she entered the cavernous mouth of the cave, almost entirely covered by thickets of dry bramble. Luckily, Veni discovered, the dry twigs crumbled at her firm touch and there were no thorns, so the whole wall of bramble came slowly apart to reveal a penumbrous space behind. She looked behind her and was nearly tempted to return to the temple, but there was a light wind at her back that pushed her forward, it seemed, almost as if the cave was sucking her in. Even as her mind was torn between going in and turning back, her body kept moving the bramble and forging ahead. The sound of the great grind inside her head receded the more she moved in. Outside, the sun became more and more remote and when she looked back, it glimmered from so far away that Veni had the feeling she was leaving everything behind. Strangely, she felt no fear and as if her feet were following some childhood trail, she had already set forth into the cave.

The rocks were rough, the sharp edges took some getting used to, but her feet too were hardened by years of playing in the sun and dirt. Bodily pain must be borne but such pain also had its limits, as her own body had shown her. Little crevices inside ourselves into which one could tuck in one's breath when the pain became overwhelming, passing vestibules of time into which you dug your nails as if into your flesh so that the immediate sting took away the dull, throbbing agony, even if only transiently, as one kind of pain bounced against another, and if you were clued into your body, you could listen to your pain and it would speak to you and you need not fear it anymore. And there's the trick with pain. She must have walked for nearly a half-hour although time inside the cave was hard to construct, save in one's mind. It might even have been an hour since she had entered. Why was she walking on and on? Some force impelled her and Veni had a presentiment that the end of the cave was near. It was the only reason for her to keep going, to get to the end, to stand there and savour what mystery there may be, to learn what she would. The place had a calming soundlessness but there was definitely some water nearby, she thought, a strange thrill flooding her heart. Her whole town ran into water scarcity every year at the height of summer and government trucks laden with water supplied the precious resource in measured amounts. For years, like many young girls born to the job, Veni had fetched water in the plastic *kudam* that was a common sight all over the state, especially in the summer months, when aquifers dried up and rivers became empty beds. Veni's ear, like that of every girl she grew up with, was thus attuned to the sounds of water and her mind now mapped these sounds in the manner of the ancient water hunters, decoding them to gauge proximity, type, even colour, all of which were necessary to determine whether the water was drinkable or not. The water sounds were making her thirsty but the belly of the cave was vast and no end seemed in sight. If she stood still and cocked her head to one side, she could, after a while, hear the pealing of the temple bells ... or just nearly. Perhaps not.

The prickly bramble had given way to thick green roots inside the cave and Veni realized that these were of trees she did not recognize. Ants and insects crawled everywhere, their noise a continuous crackle against which the vesper sounds of water stood out. A light breeze hit her face, now and then, and the air was dank with moisture. Veni's breath heaved from the walking and from anticipation – where was this path going? And just as suddenly as the bramble gave way to her exploring hands, the maze of roots and vegetation suddenly led up to a shimmering grey clearing. *Water!* Her heart leapt as it always did when, from afar, she would see the truck carrying water chug its way towards the open grounds where women and girls waited, their hair tied in colourful ribbons, and the susurrus of daily chatter gave way to excited yells and howls. All the women in her town were primed from childhood to sniff out water, and inside the cave, as the air grew more and more moist, Veni had known there was water close by.

The little pool glimmered in the low light – for a while it was all she could see, and it seemed the cave ended at the pool. She was so excited she couldn't see past the water. Veni cupped up some and brought it close to her nose. She could smell the faint aroma of earth, leaves and something indefinable. Cautiously, she took a sip, then another. She opened up her fingers to let the remaining fall back. Again, she scooped up a palmful and, this time, drank all of it. Inside her mouth, the water was a deluge of flavours – cool, sweet and earthy, it had the freshness of rainwater and the surprising sweetness of coconut water. But, wait, there was more: it had the quality of *quenching* so that every sip of it made life course through one's body, like horses galloping wild. Veni could not believe that water could taste this sweet, this satisfying. With both her palms, she repeatedly drank in, her hands splashing the pool's surface as joy streamed through her throat all the way to her very spirit. A sudden pang, the memory of tortuous days, clawed at her throat sharply: there were days when her mouth lost contact with all flavour and even water tasted of something to be chewed, so with her stitches still raw, she would attempt to move her lips, forgetful of the motion of water inside the mouth, until the sudden, tearing pain would remind her that an unmoving mouth was best. The circumstance and stagnation of those days clouded her eyes as she drew her fingers lightly on the waters of the pool, its cool ripples stirring old memories and patterns she had hoped had gone dormant.

Only the parched know the *pleasure* of water, Aatha would always say. In those days when Aatha could move about, spry as a cat, she was always surrounded by pregnant women, who would come to her with their many ailments. Aatha would put her ear to their bellies, look deeply into their eyes, pinch their skin, tickle their feet and give them cool ice water to drink, all the while talking to the young, heavy-bellied girls, gauging the cause of their aches and pains. Aatha could tell which baby was hungry and which thirsty; which were twins, which triplets (there was a famous case in the town that Aatha foresaw before sending the woman to the city hospital); which baby would like music, which dance. Aatha could tell uncanny truths. She could also tell the difficult ones and forewarn the mothers, and her warm touch and ice water – the latter she specially sourced from the truck men – kept her in perennial demand as babies were born throughout the year.

Veni thought of Aatha each time she took a sip. Amma and Aatha quarrelled a lot, but when it came to caring for the pregnant women who visited their home, they were thick as thieves. Everyone's common love was iced water and the women giggled like little girls – some, no older than fifteen or sixteen – tittering and joking as they sipped the water, as restorative as ambrosia. It was that kind of healing power Veni felt in that moment and, for a while, she forgot about the cave and the darkening light. In the days when her little one was inside her, the dogs could smell her from metres away: they came rushing to her, yelping and yowling, ecstatic, though she brought no food, as they jumped around protectively. When she walked into the classroom, the kids would throng about her and her colleagues, especially the men, would gravitate towards her for little things, for a quick chat, or to bring her a fruit. What astonishing powers nature grants to the woman's body when she carries a baby. To ward off the evil eye, Amma would put a small black dot near her neck, hidden under the chin, and she would note how beautiful Veni looked, how attractive motherhood had made her. But there were also days when Veni could barely keep any food or water in and woke up feeling haggard and worn out, although the day had barely even begun. So many demands are made upon this one body, she recalled, feeling remote from the Veni of her past. What a bewildering time it had been; had it not been for Aatha and Amma and the many women around, those months would have been confounding and torturous.

From one side of the inky pool, the water thinned out considerably and a winding path could be seen. The cave went further! Veni made to go down this path, filled with slippery pebbles, decades – perhaps centuries – of exposure to water having smoothed out their roughness and made them round, almost pliant to the feet, a thorough contrast to the jagged rocks out in the front. Taking care not to slip, Veni sucked in her breath as she skirted past the wall of the cave down the narrow path. She wondered how the pool had formed since there was no sign of water dripping from above or from the sides of the rocky corridor she had been walking along. What *was* feeding the pool?

As she moved further in, Veni felt a fan of warm, moist

air on her face. The curve of the path after the pool was such that a direct draft was not possible, and the twisting stone path led further in. She picked up her pace and just as unexpectedly as she had discovered the pool, she found herself in front of a massive opening. Sunlight poured in from a vast hole from the roof of the cave and so large was the clearing that gigantic trees grew in abundance. The sun's rays lit up the whole place and it was in astonishment that Veni realized this subterranean forest was entirely invisible from above!

By now, she had lost all sense of direction and could not fathom which part of the mountain's belly she was in. Legends passed from aatha to *pasanga*, grandmother to child, spoke of ancient kingdoms under the mountain, but Veni had always thought these to be magical tales, unlike what her science books had taught her. Amma's nighttime stories of flying waters, shining rivers and carpets of flowers all made for such vivid images in a child's mind. The paradisial forest in front of her seemed to have come out of one such tale. Her mouth agape, Veni walked into the well-lit doline in utter astonishment. Soft grass grew plentifully and a verdant carpet lay before her. Her feet, so accustomed to rocks and stone, felt the soft grass giving way under her stride. She looked about in total wonder, the majestic trees billowing gently, just like the trees above ground did. Had she walked into another world altogether? What miracle was this?

Staggered by the size of the subterranean forest, Veni tried to think of the biggest thing she had ever seen in her life. That had to be the sea, when once, as a child, she had accompanied her father and mother to Kanyakumari. She was ten at the time, her twin brothers only five. Many of her memories were of the horizon so far away that the sea seemed endless. Her little feet dug into the wet sand and the water bubbled around her toes, tickling her, pushing her off-balance. When she turned her head back towards her family, the stores dotting the beach seemed like tiny matchboxes, the tourists in them looking like dolls in a puppet show. When she looked back again at the sea, the sun seemed shockingly far away, like a small glowing *bondai*, soft and yellow and chewy like the fritters Aatha made on sultry afternoons for the hungry siblings. This cave-world was bigger than even the sea of her memories, and dumbstruck, heart soaring in joy, she widened her eyes as if to take in as many sights as she possibly could. The trees were upright like giants and some thousands of them, surely, stood in front of her. There were bushes of all kinds and grass grew abundantly. Flowers of the most amazing variety were in bloom all around. Insects and swallows flew about, and as if from a distant place, came sounds, to her utter astonishment, of monkeys! The clearing through which sunlight poured in was a luxuriant green, but where the sun did not reach, vast penumbral sections fell into thick darkness.

Something about the trees near the highest spot of the opening caught Veni's eye. She peered at them, shading her eyes against the sun, and her heart lurched as she saw the high fifty-foot-tall trees with bark bright as the colours of a rainbow. Veni recognized the leaves right away – the trees were nilagiri, with whose aromatic leaves Aatha used to make hair oil, which she and Amma then lovingly applied every week on Veni's thick hair. Aatha made the blend by boiling coconut oil and dropping into it many kinds of leaves – nilagiri, *thulasi*, *murungai*, *kariveppilai*, *malli* – which sputtered and breathed out their essences, while also adding spices like *seeragam*, *sombu*, *elakkai*, *krambu elumichai thol* that converted the mix into a heated aromatic infusion that she claimed calmed anger, made one grateful and helped hair grow strong and lustrous. Veni thought of her two mothers across the generations and the ardour and life of their warm hands as she remembered the pungent smell of the nilagiri leaves. Scraps of an Ammoovanar song that Amma would sing while oiling Veni's hair floated into her memory:

When my love,
my foaming festering frothing love,
bursts forth,
my heart slips away to him,
but when I miss him,
it returns to me right away!

Veni would often doze off while Amma and Aatha went to work on her hair, their hands magically transporting her to watery worlds far away. Something of those strange, out-of-body voyages of her childhood dreams came once more to her as she looked around in wonder at the trees. How is it possible that this nilagiri had a rainbow-coloured bark? She could not believe the sight and rubbed her eyes a few times, pinching herself on the arm to make sure she wasn't dreaming. But then, life in the cave-world had so far hardly proved normal, in any known sense of the word. The trees swayed in the wind and the leaves rustled disarmingly – it was a marvellous sight.

As she saw the light dance through the leaves of the trees, another memory snaked into her mind's eye, one from a darker time filled with pain and lamentation. She recalled the light of afternoons when she lay in her bed at home, unable to move, a heavy weight crushing her heart and torso and legs, leaving her incapable of volition, only being able to look out the window bars, as Aatha and Amma cleaned her in warm water drenched in herbs and their pious prayers. When Amma tired of her eternal vigil, Appa took over, spoon-feeding Veni some gruel and Aatha's inventive pickle, *ooruga*, made of esoteric vegetables like *narthanga*, *sundakkai,* even *kariveppu*. She ate to regain her strength and she ate to keep tears away from the eyes of her devastated parents and grandmother, but in those days, she sensed no flavours in her mouth – everything tasted as ash.

My foaming festering frothing love
... returns to me right away!

Her daydream inside the cave was halfway between a real past and an unreal present – or was it the other way round? Veni teetered on the edge separating the two. This world was real, wasn't it? Like a proud, amorous peacock puts all on display, on the gradient slope leading up to the trees, the terrain turned hilly, striking for its incredible size and spread. To reach the rainbow-barked nilagiri, one would have to go past this rough area that looked forbidding from far. Noting carefully, Veni saw several chimney-like structures similar to those near her home, which Appa said were colonies containing millions and millions of ants, especially of the fiery red variety all children were taught to be wary of. As she walked towards the large patch of land, she saw on the ground rows and rows of ants that were darting and scampering in all directions. On first sight, it looked like chaos and the ants seemed caught in the throes of a mad scramble. She noticed right away the scurrying black ant, which kids picked up to make it run all over their arms because it did not sting and only tickled the skin with its zigzag walk. Then there was the ant they called 'black butt' because it raised its backside in a peculiarly impudent way and its walk was more like a strut. There were also the tiny red ants visible only when they clustered like gossipy men on evenings in the town. And then there were the large black ants that walked in formation behind each other like army personnel guarding the lines. Veni wondered how these usually territorial creatures were cohabiting without decimating each other's communities. Squatting down to watch the world of ants in its everyday flow of life, Veni imagined herself to be a giant, blundering about on the ground, startling the tiny creatures, and she wondered how they saw her.

What if, she thought, we humans were like ants to some godlike figure who squatted among us, invisible, and watched our goings-on? Maybe this was how God worked – like an unseen colossus among infinitesimal humans. But what appeared to be a riotous scramble began, upon patient, careful watching, to take shape and form and pattern. Veni began to see labour and purpose in the miniature world. While several thousand ants were busy making more and more mounds, many others were foraging, carrying dead bodies of fellow ants and other insects. Yet more were building bridges, combining and separating to make intricate structures, all impelled by the relentless need to obey the hidden queen and to translate and communicate constantly. 'Busy as an ant' was a common expression in her tongue, but Veni only now realized the truth of the adage as she saw this megacolony behave like one large family whose heartbeat was the same and which took care of its own, hunkering down against the world to survive another day and then another and so on. To see them live their lives without heed to hers or any other's was a reminder of the need to remain active, to do, to be, and to not give up, not now, not ever. But could one be like an ant? Did ants have minds and hearts that could feel inner pain? Or does pain in complex beings become more complex? There, looking at the ants, Veni wondered about the simple things and the complex things of life, and stood cloven between the two uncomprehendingly.

The wind touched everything in the open area and

went through leaves and branches, creating one unending song. After the cacophonies at the school, the market, the grounds, even one's home, the sounds of the cave and its hidden forest were music to her ears. The grass under her feet felt alive, bearing a strange kind of energy from the ground. She bent her leg and peered at her feet, all wet and glistening from the walk. Were her eyes playing a trick or had her skin erupted into several thousands of root-like filaments that clove the grass when she pressed down? *Microvilli*, a word her father had taught her during one of their many walking conversations, floated into her head. But this must be some kind of magic or were her eyes playing tricks on her mind? Even as she was marvelling at the strange connection, the cave broke open with the din of birds. *Zreet! Zreet! Zreet!* In less than a minute thousands of birds flew out from the dark side of the cave up into the lit sky with a sound that echoed all through the universe, and Veni stood mesmerized. Her very being seemed to shiver to the wild escape as the birds flew up in a formation that defied anything she had ever seen. For the next several minutes, Veni saw the horde of birds move in unison, driven by one heart, one soul, one sound, expanding and contracting, swelling and fading, contorting as one body of a gigantic bird that could now suck in its belly, now dip its fantastical head, now rise like the notes of the song the wind was writing between the trees. The mass broke into two, then four, each swelling and receding, moving back in, splitting again, several times, like legerdemain in the sky. She stared in awe, her whole being entranced by the spectacle. Simultaneously, there rose a clamour that shattered the earlier sounds of the rocky valley – like wind escaping a tunnel, the murmuration of birds built up to a crescendo, the zreets and screeches climbing higher and higher until right at the peak, just as it had begun, so the throng scattered and in a matter of seconds, vanished from sight. For a few moments, Veni stood in utter astonishment, incapable of grasping what she had witnessed and wondering if the gods in heaven were sending her signs.

Even though the birds were gone, the echo of their wingbeats could be felt in her thumping heart. Slowly, she returned to her surroundings as her eyes scanned the skies, now bereft of the several thousand birds. How was she to share what she had witnessed? In all her years, she had never seen this phenomenon nor had Aatha or Amma or Appa ever told her about it. It felt like a benediction she had received but Veni did not know what to make of it all. The sky was turning golden slowly and life above the grotto called her back. Amma was worrying, she knew. Especially, of late, Amma only worried and fretted for all her children. Aatha's declining years, Amma's growing paranoia, Appa's hardening into a shell beneath which she could barely recognize the man who taught her so many things about the external world, her brothers, such a peculiar duo, so much like each other, so difficult to fathom what their two beating hearts saw and received as one – this was her family upon whom she had brought tragedy and all of whom bore scars for her. Veni put an unsteady hand on her trembling stomach and looked at the darkening sky. Her heart grew heavy at the thought of going back. It was as if her home were here and she was leaving to never return.

4

WHEN I FIRST SAW HER, SHE WAS WATERING THE plants in the local school. She had made a hole in a plastic kudam and was using that to sprinkle water over the flowers. It was the kind of unnecessary, uncalled for labour she was always prone to playfully agreeing to. I'm not sure what it was about Veni but her yellow *pavadai* and tight, oiled braid, and her obvious joy in tending to the plants – there was something real and earthy about her. After that, I would often try to spot her amidst the gaggle of girls in the town. She used to go for dance lessons until an accident changed all that. But before that accident, I would follow her all the way from her home to dance class and then back. She knew about me, yet did not initiate contact. And I was too dumbstruck to do it myself. Thankfully, some of my friends made it their life's mission to bring us together and, well, long story short, that's how we first spoke to each other – after a friend intervened. What do I say about Veni? There's not much a husband can say, especially after what happened. I sometimes think of the Veni before and the Veni after and my mind cannot wrap itself around what changed for me. Everything changed. But then I wonder, did it? All I know is that I am no god and I cannot forget or forgive. Some days, I go mad thinking about what happened, how she survived, *why* she survived. The Veni I taught in school with, my colleague and companion, I can say now, it is impossible to go back to that Veni, to how things were. Sometimes, when I try to remember her, I can recall many little details, but on other days, a haze falls over my time with her and I cannot figure out whether I had any time that was real, substantial, or, you know, at all with her. She was knowable in so many ways – her likes and dislikes, her walk, her smile, all these things by which we measure a person, these were so ... available. But then she had those days when she was impenetrable – what I mean is, even before ... the event, she was prone to a certain stoniness, I don't have a way of putting it other than to say, she would say something to me but I knew her mind was elsewhere. Even when we were making love some nights, I could tell her body was with me but her mind was elsewhere. Like when she was grinding rice, saree hitched up, her arms moving in rhythmic bursts with her legs splayed around the stone, but her eyes fixed on some horizon far away, and if you were saying something, she had that look where she was in some world far removed from this one, where she couldn't hear a thing you said despite sounds of agreement from her mouth. I see that you're also taking notes, so let me make it clear: I'm not saying Veni was mad or anything, but I didn't really have all of her in this marriage. Some part of her was never truly mine. Her mother thought her hair was her most attractive feature and, in fact, I think, most Tamil women think of hair in that way. I myself have modern tastes and I like women with short hair, not very short like a boy or a man, nothing unfeminine but you know, below the shoulder, with a front fringe, or some such style, and not the oiled, always-plaited braid that all these young girls adopt I don't know under what stricture, because even my Akka did this until the hard water in her husband's hometown ruined her hair so badly she had to get it cut to a manageable length; however, then the new haircut suited her well, in my opinion, although at every family function she would attach a fake braid to wear flowers. Sometimes, I think it is women themselves who do not want to break away from tradition and prefer to work within social expectations. With Veni, I always gave her the freedom to do what she liked, so long as she first discussed it with me, which she did. Or well, she did for the first few years of our marriage and then, she stopped. Sorry, you want me to speak louder? Okay, that is on? Okay, I will try. She used to call me 'yennanga' as a joke because my mother never addressed my father by name but instead uses 'will you listen?'. As a result, Veni adopted that word and intonation. But, you know, it was a comforting word for me as I had heard it all my life as a child and it reminded me of my father and mother, so although she thought it was a joke, the truth is I adored being called that way. Her voice was so sweet in those days, like warm honey, you know, straight from the hive, still throbbing with bee-heart, still coloured with sunlight. At night, she would unbraid her tresses, loosening them, because the tight plait all day long gave her a headache, she said, and I would watch her loosen everything one by one – her petticoat, her blouse, her bra – and wonder why is it that women lace themselves so tightly in so many things which then have to be undone before you can get a good night's sleep? We would laugh at such things back then, and on some nights, I would spoon her inside me or she'd cuddle me from the out and my palms rested inside her breasts, her warm cleavage like soft walls of belonging. We were so happy once upon a time, or maybe it is something about being young and curious. We shared many days of mutual knowing and playing and wandering and working together. She was uninhibited when it came to work – for a schoolteacher, she had no hesitation in donning one of my shirts and a pavadai, tying her hair in an old cotton *thundu* to start clearing away thorny bushes in order to make ground for a small garden or something. She had no fear of snakes or dangerous animals, and I used to be the one whom she had to look out for. I had no idea how to do anything with land, how to plant or water, or hack away stubborn weeds with the *aruval* – now that I think about it, I wonder if she felt protected then when I was around, in those days when things were simple and clear. Because after the er ... event, she screamed when I touched her at night and her nightmares made me wary of her constant movement, her twitching feet, her shivering body, even on hot nights. When the night tremors took over, sometimes even during the day, her fingers shook and I could see her grasp things tight, too tight, as if the glass would fall if she didn't squeeze the life out of it and her hands sometimes locked up because of how tight she squeezed things and I had to muster superhuman strength to pry things out of her hands. Some of the wounds on her face and the fractures took the longest to heal but she was uncaring of scars, so Amma applied ointments and creams and we all took turns remembering her medicines and injections. For several months after ... well, now I look back to that time and it feels like a story one saw in a film or some tale told by a visiting aunt. Was it so many months or did time slow down to an instant? What can I say? A silence yawned between us. Even after her wounds healed, two or three years later, I could not hug her anymore at night, but she did let me put a pillow between us, and in that shared space, apart, she would lie down for some ten–fifteen minutes before waking up and staring at the wall. On those nights, all I could do was be quiet and wait for her madness to pass. Some nights, I would wake up suddenly to find that she had rearranged an entire room. We had no visitors and had not purchased anything new, but she would take it into her head to move things around, including heavy tables. It is not that I did not take her to doctors; I did, and especially in those days when she stayed up all night not sleeping because she said she saw bizarre dreams, so she began to doze all day, one irregular nap at a time, but then that whole system threw everything off-balance and she began, one day, to bang her forehead with the utensils. I took her to doctors, even one psychologist, who had been referred by our town specialist and who claimed to be trained in trauma care. Trauma was a new word and concept for us, but it was helpful because Veni was coming apart in so many ways that it was impossible to run after specialists for each episode. So, this one doctor was a very good thing for us and he was fairly affordable. He said she was a special case of eidetic memory or something like that, which apparently meant it made it harder for her than for other people in similar circumstances, so he gave her things to do like imagining new places or using her memory to draw a face in the air and then describe it in words. I did not often understand the point of such exercises. Nevertheless, it was a break from the despair and tedium of sitting at home and it was a shot at doing *something*. I think we should have stuck with him but she stopped going after two or three sessions without giving me any reason. In fact, increasingly in the past four years, she stopped telling me why she would do certain things. For example, she converted our entire house into one colour – everything had to be yellow. When things like the television or a table were not yellow, she would cover them with a yellow saree or sheet. The entire house, can you believe it, *one* colour? The walls she plastered up with upside-down newspapers one day – these were her sudden kinds of madnesses. I bore it all; she was after all, my wife, but after a point, I began to wonder at the meaning of things. I became detached, you know, separate from her, looking at the things she would do, trying to understand from a place that I increasingly began to see was outside and not inside where she was. It was hard to go to public places because everyone's eyes said, we know, and I began to avoid common spaces. Instead, I found quiet spots near the school or close to the old, abandoned bus station where no one went. What? No, the old mill and its stinking road I avoided entirely – what would have been the point? I mean, you know. So anyway, I was not going to school either. The principal gave us both leave from teaching and Veni got a longer time off. I was apprehensive about returning – Adhiban and his cronies were flourishing and what was gained by it all other than making our lives hell? The police and local leaders were in their pockets and who will take the word of a woman against a man's or of us against them? It is an unfair world we live in, I know that, and I told her that, but she wouldn't listen. After several months of recovery, we were tossed from one politician to another, one NGO to another, and the media people who constantly assailed us. For a short while, Sittanavasal was the only thing on TV, but slowly, other, more sensational news took over the main screens and Veni's story became sidelined. We were given conflicting advice and all the while Veni's medical appointments and therapy swamped our life. She was obsessed with sending the five men to jail, but they used all kinds of tactics to make evidence disappear, buy the police and the judges, and turn Veni into an unreliable accuser. And then they tried to remove her from her people, burying us under volleys of abuse, calling her a prostitute and other vile names, all the while riling up the town, keeping us all on edge. It should not have been easy for them because Veni's family had such deep ties with other families but everyone was afraid and their intimidation worked. All said and done, the shame was Veni's, so who could come forward? I am an ordinary man, I come from an ordinary family – how long could we have stood against ... against all of them. Veni's manic episodes, inability to 'regain normalcy' – that's what the judge said – all went against her word. I only cared for her health, and I could see what this unequal fight was doing to her, to us, our family. In these years of relentless pursuit, what did she manage? Only to alienate us from everyone, to get sicker by the day, to forget me and that I was there too, and on top of everything, to forget that we lost a baby. I know what you are here for, but the truth is that I haven't met or spoken to her now in months. The simple truth is I do not know where she is. Things changed utterly four years ago and, try as we might, we couldn't make up for our losses. We have all paid for it, haven't we? About Adhiban, what can I say? Death keeps a calendar that no one knows. And did all this leave any of us untouched? Look at the family, each one wounded beyond recognition, damaged for life. But for what? Life goes on for everyone, doesn't it? No one truly knows the weight of another's burden. Now that I look back, there are so many things she … we could have done that may have prevented the accident, I mean, the event. I mean, I could have accepted the job in Karunagagiri and taken her along with me. Why did I agree to stay in this stupid town where her family was and where she felt comfortable? If I were a typical bridegroom, I would have put my foot down and said, my wife goes where I go. Yes, she wouldn't have a job in Karunagagiri when we went, but in the future, she would have found something – jobs are a matter of luck, of being in the right place at the right time. No, that was not to be. As things went, I was here, I had to get into the good books of Adhiban – when we first met him, he was so concerned and eager to help; he said he would speak to someone to get me a job in the same school as Veni – and from thereon, I was fated to enter the school Veni was teaching in. I mean, I look back in time and there itself, that moment, when I decided to find a job and settle in Sittanavasal, I was doomed. I could have gone to my father's godforsaken birthplace, a village only, but no, I had to choose otherwise. I could have gone to Chennai, or even as far as Bhopal, you know, where Saravanan from the house near the junction – you know him? – he went to Bhopal for a job. I mean, a job could have taken me anywhere in this big world, but I was not really running after any job and thought I would just be where Veni was. So, you see, I was fated to be in Sittanavasal. If I had known what I now know, I would have done things so differently. After that first play, life was a series of chess moves and perhaps, our defeat was inevitable. Everything that happened was inevitable. But for that decision to sit down and play on this board, and not that board, our whole life may have been completely different. I keep thinking back to the events of our life as one long stream where, at different points, we meet different people who change the course of our lives completely. So it is that Adhiban came into our lives and I joined the local school to work alongside Veni, a simple enough event that was to have long-range effects on our family as Adhiban wormed his way into our lives and brought his contacts and friends, joining our existence with his. These connections of life, how do we understand them? Was it friendship and then betrayal? No. We were never big enough, socially upward enough to be his friends. It was merely a matter of our intersecting circles of life – there was no inherent reason for our acquaintance. If we had not met Adhiban, we may not have come inside the circumference of his life, and then, perhaps Veni may have been spared the great misfortune that befell her and me. We are all, in so many ways, fated to live through one of many possibilities in our life: which one, we cannot always foresee, and only in the evening of our lives, with sufficient sorrow in our souls, do we manage to see glimmerings of the full picture of one's existence. Every why has a wherefore, our elders say, don't they. In one of my many meanderings, I met a *sannyasi* who said to me that each person we meet in life is a point of no return, a turn away from a possible future to another possibility, and the illusion of choice – the notion that we choose one path – is our necessary friend in life. Without the illusion of freedom and choice, we would merely die in terror of fate's hidden ambushes, hiding behind every hairpin turn in life, crouching under each rock about to dislodge upon our heads. So it is that I think this was all fated to be. What else explains it all, you tell me? What else ... Well, I have turned, as you can see, to philosophy and meditation to understand how one can live with the agonies and disappointments of one's life. I used to be a teacher of mathematics – I sought in numbers the patterns of our daily life, but now I understand that numbers are hardly patterns, merely shadows of patterns that elude our understanding so long as we are far from death. The closer we get to dying, the more intimately we can see the patterns of our living – it is, what they call, a paradox. What did you say? No, I do not know what she is doing or what her plans are. I too heard that she was seen walking off with Adhiban's head. I don't know if that was her.

People say it was a short-haired person in a saree – I mean, a man could dress like a woman, no? But what can I say? I don't stay in Sittanavasal anymore. In fact, I do not stay long in any one place – too many shadows that creep along. I will say one thing though: the Veni I knew would never cut her hair. So, I don't think this was her; it's a story for everyone, and to each his own version. Me, I don't think she did it. Whoever did has struck terror into the hearts of the other four alive. I bet they keep thinking they are next and perhaps a living death, day by day, little by little, is just the kind of punishment for them after all. But I don't want to rake up the past. Everything is known. You will find all the details in newspapers and police records. So, what is there to add by way of 'my story'? It is not my story anyway, it is Veni's – go find her and ask. I worry that Adhiban's friends turned against him and have now made Veni disappear too. Have you looked into that angle?

5

I AM NOT SURE WHAT YOU THINK CAN BE GAINED by coming here to speak with me. I am a broken man, this world has broken me and my daughter, and now the stories circulating about her are enough to strike terror in a father's soul. As if we have not lived in darkness for the last four years, there is this burden to bear too. What can a father say other than to beat his chest or tear his hair as a public spectacle of his defeat, his failure to protect his child? But I will not do so. I am not made that way. My Veni was a little butterfly, like that little yellow one that flits about the weeds? She was like that as a child in her yellow pavadai and sweet braided hair, flouncing about. She was curious and diligent in listening when I told her stories about flies and moths and larvae and cocoons. Even as a child, she was unafraid of animals and insects;

while her other little friends fretted about and feared holding toads, millipedes and birds, she would love to get her hands into the soil and walk the bushes and thickets looking for little chameleons or turtle eggs in the sand or owlings in the trees. I nurtured this fearless love of nature in her, because what are we humans if not a part and parcel of our environment? I like to think her love of geography came from my training her to be a nature lover and an adventurer seeking her own answers. I was forced by the compulsions of my life to not follow academics, to become a factory man, but to her, I passed on my love of knowledge, facts, trivia. It was a happy day in our family when Veni became a schoolteacher, but little did we know that behind that joy loomed a great shadow, the blackest of all shadows. But how could we have known? How could anyone? Now, you are here to talk about her but what I can say that will be of any use to you? No, but I want to speak my side of things and I hope this recorder of yours will hold my Veni's story longer than your courts could. So yes, I was saying that she followed in my ways, that she was such an unusual spirit – as a child, as a teenager, as a young woman. To you, she is a number on a file, a headline, an accused, but beyond that, little else. Getting to know that much about her is sufficient; any more is unnecessary. But I am her father and for me, every little thing about her is vital, indispensable to knowing her. If you must understand her, I will have to tell you of the time she and I talked about tribes like the Padaei and the Fore, who are known to cannibalize their old and sick. From our local library in Pudukottai, we looked up books about diseases like *kuru* that such tribes suffered from and Veni was curious about the community's rationale behind their unusual practices – I did not know the answers to her questions. Do you? Would you have the answers to any of the questions my daughter might raise? Stay for a while. Stay for as long as my stories last, but tell me, what would be the point? You have ears but where is your soul to listen to the stories I have to tell? You have only come for one thing and it is the one thing I cannot provide. I simply do not know where she is. I have not had answers for a long time now. Even when she was in front of me, walking, talking, listening, eating, sleeping – not so much for the past many months, just barely – even in all these everyday activities that I hoped were healing her, little by little, I did not know her. To one such, you bring your futile questions. All I can say is that this home was hers and she was here, and she thrived here and died inside its walls even when she was alive. What those brutes did to her took away her heartbeat and what then remained was a set of organs merely living out the remainder of its predestined time. Does this sound melodramatic to you? Then what can I say. I am a man of few words and have rarely known or shown great passion. My life has been led in measured outcomes and I was very happy in this world. My mother, my wife, my daughter, my sons – what more does a man want? My job at the iron foundry involved shaping metal into form and as a foreman, I had a great team of men to work with. Work nourished me, put food on the family table, and gave me a reason to live for others. What free time I could find, I read about rocks and planets, oceans and ancient travel routes, bees and beetles – I wasn't very picky so long as the topic was tied to our natural world. This is an average life, is it not, and we were all so happy in it, I like to think. My wife and my mother had their tiffs, but who doesn't enjoy a little domestic drama? On most days I was out of the house; however, I knew well how my mother and wife looked after pregnant women who visited our home for help and care. When I returned in the evening, the place would reek of oils, herbs, spices, and all around, there were towels made out of old sarees and sheets, both our own and those donated by various other households, that Amma had repurposed. The laundry alone in the house ran up to quite a penny, but both women laboured hard with two or three other townswomen to make sure the clothes used for the care of expecting mothers were always clean and germ-free. In my own small way, I would contribute by not questioning my wife when she took money out of our household expenditure to buy things for the medical care of those who came to our home. What a time that was. Amma's reputation as a midwife was legion around these parts – I was always a proud son, prouder yet of my daughter who imbibed so many of the great qualities my mother has. My sons showed disregard towards academics and were obsessed with cricket, both of them, just as children should be, I suppose. Aatha's tales of valour, our old poems of *mañcuvirattu* and *jallikattu*, about young herders competing for the hands of slender maidens filled their head with childish dreams. At night, when I checked in on the boys, I would find them mock-fighting with garlands made of coconut leaves or newspapers and make-believe swords, one pretending to be the great black bull running pell-mell to avoid capture, and the other twin playing the youthful herder trying to bring the bull under control and assert his dominance. Amma's old song would come to my mind then:

My heart trembles to see the herder wearing a kāyā garland.
He attacks a red bull that charges at him
with everlasting strength, seizing its ears,
like Thirumāl who tore open the mouth of a maned horse
sent by his enemies.

I would watch the two rascals put up this pantomime, their childlike immersion in old legends moving me beyond measure, until awareness of my presence broke the idyll and both boys, sheepish at being discovered, readied for sleep. This was our life: ordinary, routine, perhaps even mediocre. I nurtured no dreams of greatness, nor did I encourage it in my children – what for? Life is for happiness, that is our greatest good, and one can find happiness in the humblest of things. Becoming rich, or owning big things, being the best at something – I never saw virtue in such goals and I was fine with my children simply being who they were and slowly, happily becoming who they wanted to be. My world was anchored in this small life, filled with small needs and small dreams. When you have lived my small life, you are supposed to remember the good and the bad, the shocks and the joys with equanimity. And equanimity is what I taught my children – Veni, most of all, my little *karuvacci*, her dark, beautiful face that could light up at the sound of a *mridungam*, resilient as ever, she changed her life's dream overnight when an accident damaged her legs forever. A father remembers everything and tucks it all deep into his chest – that is his curse. Perhaps I was setting myself up for tragedy; perhaps I should have taught my children – and learned myself – how to guard against the extraordinary, the catastrophic, the fire and the storm. Perhaps knowing the frogs, bees and birds took too much time away from her training, and my daughter never learned the important things: how to stand up, how to fight, how to cut, wound, maim, kill, how to protect herself. I must have failed because surely there are things a father must do, for the child is but blank paper and we write whatever we write on it and they only continue what we begin and what I wrote was so useless, so utterly, utterly useless that she had nothing to build on. What good has the knowledge of the mayfly brought to her, when I could have taught her how to use an aruval to swing and slice? What good came to her for knowing the different kinds of darkness in the night? I should have taught her instead how to pound a man's brain. Isn't that so? I could ... should have taken the time to teach her these things and I taught her instead about stars and rain and the moving comets. Stupid things that filled her head with ideas, leaving no room for the stuff of life, for the things a girl must have in order to survive in our world. What is it our ancient poems sang of? Of young, virile men receiving maidens as rewards for their masculinity, but what of the young maidens – what choice did they have?

There,
the man who lies on the neck of the white bull will get
the pretty young woman with well-set teeth,
the man who seizes the sharp-horned black bull without
fearing its rage will sleep with the pretty young
woman with combed hair, wearing bright jewels,
the man who subdues the murderous bull with coloured
eyes will get the young woman with pretty eyes and looks
of a bewildered deer, and the man who captures the
tough red bull with fierce rage will sleep in the
delicate, bamboo-like arms of the young woman wearing
striped earrings.

When my children heard these songs, did they look past the ancient drama between man and animal to the other tale, the embedded tale, which too was one of brutal dominance, of silence and capture? Why blame my boys for something I too never noticed until my own daughter fell prey? Why blame my sons or the townsfolk who could see in my Veni's ruin only shame and dishonour brought upon me and my family name, and for no fault of hers other than that of being born a woman? What honour do they speak of? My daughter's broken body far outweighed the lie and illusion of honour that this society peddles to us. The only honourable life is one that is free from the control of another. My honour, my family's honour is not secreted away in the organs of my children. It has not been besmirched by my children's tragedies but the failures of my country and its rulers. I look at my children and think what is it that one loses when a child is gone? What is a life? Is it the number of years you are alive? Is it the number of times you recall having played with your child? Or is it the unnumbered memories that assault you in your child's absence? Is it the thought of the thousands of possibilities that vanish in an instant? A parent is the most pathetic of all creatures in the world because every breath of his, his heartbeat, his dreams, they have gone out of his body and scattered into the faces, smiles and souls of his children and he must live, always half in terror, at the brute prospect of his child's vanishing. When you are a father, you forget to sleep permanently. But what good came of my wakefulness anyway? Amma used to say Veni has the siddhi in her but a girl needs more than siddhi to make her way in our world. I could have been the author of a whole chapter of her life where she learned what would protect her. Instead, I wasted that time and I didn't realize it then but I brought on her and my family the fire that has now torched my home and scorched our bodies so we do not recognize who we are anymore. My sons are madmen, their language is a mystery the world cannot unlock – have you seen the two brothers? I, their father, have let them down too. The other day I wanted to sit with them, have a meal like any father would, ask them about their day, tell their mother to fetch the paper so we could discuss it, but instead, when I saw them, I walked past and went into my room impotently. Perhaps they rightly blame me, and I can see in their burning eyes the choking accusation that embers within them and never dies. How do they go about town, these young men left with scorched skins and faces and memories, only the haziest, most distant memories, of a different life? I can meet no one's eye now, let alone my daughter's, for what can a man, who so clearly failed in the most important duty of his life, say to his daughter that will cover up for his thorough failure? If you are looking for someone to blame, forget my daughter, your search can stop. I am here, and you can take me to jail, to try and understand the tatters of this family's life. I am at the back of it all, although I barely knew it, hardly sensed that I was failing my daughter all this while, little by little, habit by habit. I sought to envelop her in the knowledge of the knowable world, and I completely disregarded the world of unknowable wills and forceful passions and unstoppable storms. Why was I not preparing her for the worst? Why was I not readying her for walking on fire? Now I sound like a crazed lunatic, so I do not speak my thoughts to others, not to my wife or my sons. Have you seen my youngest? Did you hear what happened? Where do I put these sorrows? Whose ear will hold my howls of silent pain? Perhaps we have all become unhinged, deranged in a world where cruelty piles upon cruelty, where fathers beat their chests for dead children, and the old never die, never escape. And most wretched of us all, my daughter, whom people in the town call mad, and I will not blame them. Even her husband, I suspect, thinks so. Where is he anyway? I heard that he has skipped town and lives like an itinerant, lurching about hotels and bars – where does he go? When does he return, no one knows. This, too, is a kind of madness, no? And of her two brothers, what do I say? They are in the grip of a folly that defies understanding – the younger one has crossed over into a world where no one can reach him, while the elder skulks through life, his hunched shoulders carrying catastrophe like a mountain. I watch them all, wordlessly, our family splintering down upon each other, crumbling into itself, trapping us all inside. This is how we say we protect each other, but it is a prison. Don't think though I do not know the part I have played in this drama. I am the reason that Veni is mad, I am the cause, at the back of it all, and there is a long way behind this one event, a long, meandering way which leads back to the father, me, who taught her nothing and failed her and turned her insane. Yes, we tried to get help but by then, the fire had razed everything. We took her to doctors who prescribed medicines in the early days right after the attack, when all she was having, it seemed, was fistfuls of tablets and water. Her mouth, she complained in those comatose days, was woolly and she couldn't taste anything. The stitches in the lower part of her body took months to fully heal, bursting open when she turned in her fitful sleep, oozing sepsis once when we had to rush her to hospital again, and slowly, under the assault of steroids, drying into scabby scars so, during the hot days, sometimes she was wildly scratching herself below, nearly ripping off the barely healed skin, driven to a feral madness as if someone had brushed her with poison ivy. Her wounds were beyond any pain I could have taught her to endure but even the recovery outmatched anything I could do to safeguard her. For a while, it was I who fed her because her mother was distracted into a stupor, cleaning up after Aatha, cooking for the home and tending to Veni. Her lip, a part of which one of them had bitten off, had to be stitched up, so for a long time, she could barely open her mouth beyond a little bit for food taken from the narrow end of a wooden spoon and water sipped through a straw. When I tell you these things, it is hard to swallow, no? Perhaps all fathers should teach their daughters to stitch up their mouths and eat and drink from the slightest of openings. Necessary training for survival, you know. Like we send boys to the army to make them men, we should send young girls to camp where they learn how to prevent being raped and, if raped and left to die, how to get up, clean off, stitch themselves together, and become normal again. You can wipe that look off your face. I hope you will never have a daughter because what is worse than not being able to protect her is teaching her endlessly to defend herself, worrying always whether you have missed something, that one thing that one day would mean the difference between her life and her living death. Was it my daughter, you ask, who walked with that barbarian's head and strode off into the sunset? I hope to God it was and like our ancient heroes, maybe one step beyond them too, she took that head and ate it and then shat it out in some place where it finally did a little good as it merged with the soil and became a part of some natural thing. There, that is my testimony.

6

HER HEART POUNDED IN FEAR EVERY TIME SHE LEFT the cave – what if she could not return? Nonetheless, she did and her feet became surer with each return. Veni had begun to come into the cave more frequently, climbing all the way to the temple first. The women thought she was turning religious. And perhaps, she was. If religion was about knowing the right path to take, then her visits to the cave were showing her the paths she was meant to take. Who would she like to be today? A bird, maybe, or a big fish.

Time had seemed like an eternity the first time she had gingerly walked into the cave. Now, it flew by, as Veni resolutely strode in. She knew exactly where was going today. She wanted to climb a rock point that she had seen the last time she was in the Garden – which, in her head, is what she had begun to call the clearing in the doline.

The way up the sharp rock face passed through a grey stretch that seemed completely desolate, in total contrast to the Garden. Veni was determined to explore that patch of land today. She arrived with a cloth bag slung across her shoulders, repurposed from an old saree, containing a small packet of food and a bottle of water. She also brought along some red thread left over from Amma's needlework, which might come handy if she got lost. The girls in Appa's stories always showed forethought like this, and Veni thought she was being quite bright. Aatha's bright one – the little star that shone the brightest, Aatha would say, especially after a hard day's work tending to the pregnant women, while Amma brought coffee and Veni massaged Aatha's aching feet. And though it was no time for sleep, Aatha would hum an untimely lullaby, whose words had embedded themselves in Veni's mind forever and which she recalled whenever she was pensive.

Sleep, little one, for day is gone,
and you must learn what Night brings:
she has come with jasmine and cereus
to say, it is time, it is time.
So, sleep, little one, sleep,
and pay your visit to the moon of dreams.
Hush, little one, hush and sleep.

Close your eyes and you will see Night
by your bedside, she's humming
your mother's song tonight.

Veni recalled the little brown-and-white cat always hugging the corridors of the school, the darling of the little children, who thronged to play with it during recess, feeding it bits from their lunches and constantly petting it, lavishing it with love and attention. When classes were over and the horde of children dispersed to their homes, Veni would stay back some days to complete official work like clearing attendance records and such, and the tabby would slink by her room then, mewling in that low voice that mimicked a child's cry. When she imagined her lost baby, it was always that sound which first came to her mind, a low whine grieving the life it had never had.

She went past the little pool, placid until her playful hands plunged into the surface and rippled it all over. Quickly, she emptied her bottle on the side and filled it with the pool's clear water. With no time to lose today, she walked swiftly to the verdant garden, waiting, as it were, for her to return. The flowers looked even more profuse than the last time, but she was determined to head in further. The rock face looked massive from afar but Veni's expert eyes – from a lifetime spent growing around arid regions – had quickly mapped a way up. But before she could get to the great rock, she had to manoeuvre herself past a large patch – the size of the local football ground in her town – which looked thorny, forbidding.

That such a patch lay in close proximity to the lush garden was itself a mystery. As Veni drew nearer, she was surprised to see a thin strip of land, like the moon's halo, between the garden and the dry zone, a space where old, rotting trees had become a haven for white, brown and yellow mushrooms of all sizes and shapes. Veni peered closely and picked one of the stems – an evanescent white and brown thing, so incredibly soft and fragile and yet robust in its own fashion. A slender brown stem with a light brown cap on which several droplets of dew rested. Veni wiped it clean on her saree and took a nibble. She was careful because mushrooms can be tricky and when you are unsure, it is best to leave them be. It tasted benign and rather watery, like an overripe berry past its prime, but its texture was a strange kind of meaty that she did not expect. Veni took a bigger bite and there it was, a definite smoky, meaty flavour she had never encountered in any of the mushrooms she had picked near her school, where they grew in abundance, and children had to be warned against foraging mindlessly. She picked up a few more stems, wiped them clean, and folded them softly in some paper in her bag. It was time to move on and as she crossed the liminal zone, Veni became aware of a distinct change in the environs. The soil grew drier and harder as she walked further towards the great rock and dry bramble; old weeds, shrivelled-up roots covered the ground, trapping the carrion of various small animals and birds. A curious quiet lay upon the place – here, even the monkeys' screeching grew so faint as to be virtually inaudible. She walked through the dried long stems of old grass, carefully avoiding the scattered bones of the animals, through the profusion of variously sized fungi, and suddenly, her eyes were looking at a massive tree several metres away. It was completely dried up, the very symbol of death if ever there was one. As she climbed the ground now leading higher towards this inexplicable tree, her breath came in quick and shallow. She turned about and from the sloping gradient, viewed the land attentively. The whole place was, in fact, a Grove of the Dead – what else could one call this derelict, wild space, and Veni stopped her trek, looking with alarm at the death and decay that surrounded her.

Soon, though, her ears picked out sounds – light crackles of beetles and worms and other insects, small rats even, the chirrup of toads, even the light hiss of a snake. The doline's omnipresent wind was still whispering.

Although everything *looked* dead, there were all kinds of familiar and unfamiliar sounds – which ones were real, which imaginary, Veni wondered. Slowly, it dawned on her that what seemed like a dead place was, in fact, abuzz with life as nature found ways to rewild the land with new species of bush and bird, soil and air. The Grove of the Dead felt like a sacred space in the cave-world and Veni, who had found herself dumbstruck by the profusion of life in the Garden, now became speechless on facing the reparative powers of death. Once her father brought home a doctor's stethoscope to show her and the boys. They heard in delight the sounds of each other's hearts and whispered gibberish into each other's ribs. Then, their father had an idea, and he took them outside. Holding the chestpiece against some soil, he put the tips into little Veni's ears. At first, she heard nothing, so tight the rubber felt against her tiny ears, but soon, upon focusing, she began to hear noises in the soil: crackling, scraping, munching, clicking, rustling – a whole soundtrack that her father called 'the song of the soil' and which, he taught her, was sign of a land's biodiversity. Standing in the Grove, she found her ears thrill to a very similar sound, although ostensibly, to shallow eyes, the place looked dead. The tree at the centre of the Grove cast a spell on everything, its heavy trunk marked by age and time, Methuselah from Aatha's stories where she mixed tales from the Bible that old missionaries had brought to their land's shores with the legend of the astonishing princess Scheherazade who told stories to stay alive. Veni remembered these mythical tales of her childhood even as all her senses took in the sights and smells and sounds of the Grove. She must walk through it in order to reach the base of the rock that she meant to climb.

Tentative as the Arabian princess before she began a tale, Veni set out slowly. What she feared, she did not know. As she walked forth on the dry soil of the grove, her trepidation waned as did her thrall to her own adventure, like the princess, she imagined, who grew surer of her strategy with every word she uttered, every story she spun. Flies and gnats, which bothered everyone so much in the upper world, flew right past her face and hair without bothering her in the least. With increasing confidence, Veni walked towards the tree, all the while carefully avoiding the carrion and the dead around, her toes gripping the cracks. Where the Garden had felt like a carpet of soft, wet petals, the Grove was a hard surface, *karisal bhoomi*, she thought, hot and dry land, but her feet felt just as sure as they did in the Garden. She avoided the long thorns of the dry vegetation, which bore bright red fruit like small pearls. That fruit was scattered everywhere the eye could see and especially near the massive tree, so gnarly from the bottom up. When she reached its base, Veni put her hand to the bark gently and to her surprise, felt a kind of pulsing energy emanate from it. As if stung by electricity, as when sometimes while ironing Appa's shirt, Veni's index finger would suddenly crinkle from a shock, her hand drew back from the strange power she felt in the tree. Was it dead or alive?

She looked up to see how the tree looked like above her. Some of its thickest branches were low and nearly straight, while others were vertiginously crooked and formed a thick web. The highest she could go, were she to climb it, would still not take her to the centre of the tree and Veni, who was a nimble tree climber, decided not to risk it at that moment. She peered closely at the tree, and an abundance of life greeted her eyes. The knobby, shrivelled-up tree, was, in fact, a microworld, a teeming depot of small insects, organisms, fungi and much else. Beetles and their larvae proliferated all over the tree, living off the various layers of its bark, feeding venously the water and nutrients that ran through it. Large parts of the lower branches were covered in moss and lichen rich with food for varieties of insects, and in the upper reaches of the tree, Veni spied several cavities that she surmised must be the home of little birds and owls looking to nest and roost. If the tree were to be brought down, as dried-up trees in her town often were, it would decimate thousands of other creatures for which it was shelter, year after year after year. Veni walked around the tree a few times to get a sense of its girth and age, awestruck that something so ancient could be so alive. If Time was kept by trees, her whole life would be the snap of a finger or maybe a single toot of a bird. In tree time, the world would be interpreted so differently than the way men putting themselves at the centre of the planet measure time. Her head spun and as the light filtered through the dry branches, Veni could see spots of colour as if a prism was scattering light all about her. It took some effort to reorient her thoughts, for today, she could not afford to get lost in a vacant mood, and with one final glance, Veni slipped past the ancient sentinel, striding towards the giant rock's base.

The pearly red fruit squished under her feet and a peculiar pink sap oozed from them, staining her feet, leaving pale footprints behind on the dry, cracked surface. As children born in proximity to the wild discern early in their lives, Veni knew not to taste wild berries or fruit, especially those that looked attractive. She picked up one of the red berries and squeezed: the pink sap was unguent and the seeds inside were a bright blue. She had never seen the likes of it. She smelled the fruit and, there again the indefinable odour she had encountered at the pool. She wondered if the red fruit had somehow made its way into the pool, but what was this strange smell she couldn't put her finger on? With a start, she realized that in the cave, her sense of smell had come back to her. In the aftermath, one of the things to happen to her – she had told Raji this – was that she could only remember some smells, which she repeatedly found in other things. For instance, one evening she began to smell a kind of old sambar stink in her home's walls, which turned so sickening that one night she decided to plaster the walls up in newspapers. Everyone knows that newspapers have a great scent that covers up the bad ones. Another time, she threw out all the pillows in her bedroom because they stank of an unwashed man, but then, oddly enough, that smell also permeated other things in the house, so she began to cover up various pieces of furniture in whatever old clothes and bedsheets she could find. This was a strange, medically mysterious period in her life, with disparate, disconnected dots for which she frequently failed to account. She had met some doctors then – so well-intentioned – but really, there was so much work to be done and so little time. Each sense of her body, every cell of her being, each breath had to be reset, and she had to be up for it. Aatha said to draw on the siddha in her and she believed that Veni would know how to minister to herself, but in her own time. With the pain came the madness; when the pain left, the madness brought the long sorrow of dispossession; when the sorrow began to abate, her memories fragmented; and as she put her memories back together, her voice faltered and her sense of smell began to leave her. Everything was a connected step in a long, heavy chain of being and Veni spent much of her day refuting a slow death, choosing to be alive. Life is too full of consequence and to lose a thread somewhere or to miss a beat, it all amounted to something, eventually. And then there was the work, the effort and exertion and toil of getting better, and looking with a smile at one's loved ones, especially on days when she woke up not remembering what the colour of a leaf was called while, on others, she couldn't smell a thing. Sorrow came in so many forms: did not a sparrow's woe have the same magnitude as a mother's anguish? Who could answer this question but the sparrow and the mother? Veni's mind ran in circles with her thoughts, expanding and contracting, but always moving, while her body remained immobile on her convalescent bed. Here, however, inside this grotto, new things were afoot and Veni could feel her mind and body realigning, like two hands on a clock finding their common rhythm: inside the cave, she could smell just alright! The leaves smelled like leaves, the water like water, and the red fruits were so delicately aromatic.

Cautiously, Veni bit into one side of the fruit – instantly, her tongue puckered at the tartness, reminiscent of the *kalakai* and *kodikkapuli* she would have with her friends. She instinctively reached out for the bottle of water and no sooner had she taken a sip than her mouth became awash with the nectarine sweetness of a pineapple or a mango. *Appa!* What magic was this? Veni took another small bite of the fruit, this time more flesh, less rind, and again, the puckering tang of it curled up her whole mouth. But the residual sweetness of water remained as the fruit hit her palate and when she took a sip of water once more, she felt the radiating delight of a sweet juice all over again. It was as if the water brought to the red berry an implausible purity and union of opposite tastes and flavour. That her mouth could feel this carnival of flavours was already a wonder, for she still nursed a scar on the side of her cheek where flesh had torn open and doctors had stitched her lip in an upward-curving arc. Veni often found herself touching the palpable scar especially when her mind was preoccupied or contemplating something, the scar a visible reminder, as in other parts of her body, of a haunting evening, a terrifying night.

This cave-world's delights are unending, Veni thought, and she picked up a few of the red fruit lying about, washed them lightly in the pool water she had bottled, and pocketed them in the hem of her cotton saree. She walked forth to the base of the rock whose face she had seen from the other side. Veni had feared that the rock would be unclimbable but to her sweet surprise, she found that, in fact, through a series of grooves and ledges, it was possible, with care and perseverance, to climb it. Hitching up her saree in the age-old, time-tested way that so many women before her had as they went about the business of daily life, Veni began to climb. The rock itself was a massive wall of limestone that had hardened over the centuries, but with rain, natural cavities had emerged all around its surface, leading to softly eroded holds that Veni's hands and feet could find a grip in. The leeward side of the rock, where she was climbing, also had generous amounts of algae, and these slippery spots Veni took care to avoid.

The rock took on odd shapes in different places: sometimes, there were deep-running cracks that looked like grooves zigzagging all the way to the centre of the massive structure, while other striations ran diametrically across, like the lines on a hand that traced one's destiny. Even as she heaved and reached upwards, Veni wondered at the rock's age – how much time had it witnessed?

Beneath the human world, secreted away in this rarest of rare spaces, what stories could it tell? Veni thought of the monastery and temple above: surely the monks knew of this world and hid it deliberately from the society of humans?

She looked down as she stood on a narrow ledge to catch her breath. She had climbed a fair way up but was not dizzy. There was half the distance left to cover, and she took a sip of water from her bottle. Again, the sweet pulse of the pool found a way to invigorate her from within – what was this magic! – and Veni went back to climbing. Ever so often, the rock's formal features struck her as curious. She had already seen star-like and snail-shell formations on the surface, as if someone had etched them into the limestone. Or was she imagining it all? As she climbed higher, she came across what could only be called coral shapes, the kind Veni had seen whenever she made a trip to the sea. She wondered if long ago, the rock had actually been part of the sea's bed with its coral and algae, now lifted high above sea level by some unseen force deep in the belly of the earth by which the ancient seas had been transformed into land.

Growing up, she had always heard tales of Kumari Kandam, the great lost continent of the Indian Ocean, on which a magnificent Tamil civilization had flourished before a catastrophe wiped out the landmass. According to Aatha, Kanyakumari, her favourite sea spot, was at some point in deep time a great city in Kumari Kandam. If Aatha's tales had any truth, Veni thought, then is it too far to think that this rock too at one point was beneath the ocean and rose up one day, just like the great continent was once upon a time swallowed by the waters? There were tales so deep and so embedded in the universe's consciousness that human beings could only imagine them using the barest of signs, Veni reasoned, like the etchings on this rock. Perhaps long before time, these sea creatures were alive and left behind their shadows graphed on the rock for Veni, on a day like today, to read.

In the cave-world, all stories were true, and all truths were stories. In the world above, only lies and deceptions ruled. Veni tried to stay in the climb, to not recall the world above, the sufferings it had wrought upon her, perhaps nothing in comparison to what women and men have borne and lived through since the earliest times. And yet, today, she longed for her lost child. Who would she have been if she had grown up? Would she have Appa's tall mien or her brothers' funny way of puckering their noses when they concentrated on their notebooks? Her husband's slightly squinty eye – would she have some of that? From Aatha, what would she have had? But what if it were a boy? Men are so strange – how would she raise a boy? Veni smiled. He might have had Amma's quiet strength. And what of her would have lived on? The child was just over four months old when she had lost it and, of that calamitous evening, as she walked past the old mill, she still remembered vividly the golden light of the sky. In the ancient past, poets called that time of the day *gowdhuli mughurtha* – that golden hour when the hooves of the cows going home threw up the dust such that light filtered through in an iridescent yellow, touching everything and dousing the world with colour and buoyance. And then, all of a sudden, everything would just hang, as if the hours had fallen off the face of a clock, holding time in abeyance, waiting, but for what? Some rain, perhaps, that would settle all that flying dust and souse the cows in the splendour of life. Veni had then imagined the gowdhuli inside of her, a little golden speck turning into a memory of the beauty and possibility of life. Later, after the attack, when she lay drenched in the blood of her unborn child, Veni clung steadfastly to the golden image of its memory and the first words coming out of her damaged mouth spurting through her blood, as she looked at her brother Chinna's face, through a fog of shock and pain, calling out for her child, to her gowdhuli.

Her eyes brimmed over and as the tears came, a light drizzle began to fall, causing her to look up into the sky.

Squinting against the sun, she noticed that a cloud shaped like a saucer had formed in the sky of the cave and was now opening up ever so slightly. Round and flat and vast in its spread, it seemed to both move and be still, as if a ferment from within was about to burst upon the entire place. From her aerial vantage, she could see the Grove of the Dead and as raindrops fell on the dry, cracked soil, the land seemed to heave a sigh. For a while, the largely arid grove soaked up the water. And then the light rain began building up and Veni knew she could not lose another minute as the limestone rock too began to become wet and slippery. She started her climb in earnest once more, and this time she was focused on reaching the top. At some holds, the rock crumbled, and had it not been for the fairly gentle gradient of the rock face, Veni might have slipped and fallen. As it was, the rock, it seemed, actively assisted her in climbing and in about ten minutes or so, Veni was nearly at the top. Here, she found root-ropes of varying lengths emerging from the top of the rock and wondered if there was a tree above whose prop roots, like the banyan, she had managed to find. Her eyes narrowed at the orb of light in the sky, now peeking from behind the cloud, now breaking open on its own, and she thought she saw the world in so many colours, the rain prismatically breaking open her reality.

As she used the roots to lasso herself upwards, she became aware that the rain had turned intense. In that limited space, vast as it was, water fell in volleys of concentrated force, as if bent on hammering open the soil. The tropical Garden had enough vegetation to absorb the cloudburst, Veni thought, but the Grove was an arid spot with no trees, save old Methuselah, shrivelled up but somehow alive in its own way. The tree reminded her of Aatha for she intuited that just like Aatha took care of the women in the town, in some mystical way, this ancient tree was also the custodian of the cave, holding in its body the balance between life and death that is the fulcrum of all existence, and especially in this cave, where all fantastical things seemed to lead up to this primordial being. Climbing the rock gave Veni a fuller perspective on how immense the tree was, its leafless branches thick with life and vitality, even as her hands felt about the rock's surface, so visceral and tactile, such that each time she explored the surface and caught a groove, it was as if she, in an explosion of vision, was feeling the face of a giant. Her eye went to some more coral etchings and algae on the sides of the rock. She put her hand on top of one of the markings and the star-like shape looked like an alien being's open palm. As the rain pounded down, there was little time to contemplate the figures; she was nearly there. With a final heave and pull, Veni clambered on top of the flat head of the rock, a massive height that gave her a panoramic view of the doline. Her breath stopped. She could not believe what she saw – the cave was beyond any size she could even conjure up in her mind. Nearly infinite, its edges were the verge of her own vision, even from the aerial vantage. She could see the lush Garden clearly now; further ahead, there seemed to be another chain of dark caves, larger than the one she had entered from, and right below, the Grove now preternaturally moist and dark. The cloud was unusual – the saucer-like shape opened up in a limited space, so that standing atop the rock, Veni was at the outer limits of the cloud. It was the first time she had witnessed a cloud limit, such that in that narrow space between pouring rain and no rain, she stood on the great rock capable of being, simultaneously, in both spaces at once.

She thought of the little boys and girls in her class; what would they say if they saw this world, its myriad beauties, its seemingly endless magic? How precious everything was! Like the soul of a child – all promise, all hope. Unbroken by the world's pain, pure spirit, pure rain, a flower, a leaf, a star, a life. The thought broke something inside Veni's pounding heart and she let out a cry which reverberated through the valley. Again, she screamed, this time, to the edge of hoarseness, and then again, tears flowing down her face, now grimy from the exhausting climb and wet from the spray of rain. Arms outstretched, Veni screamed repeatedly and wailed as loudly as her lungs would permit. Time stopped. There was only the sound of her infinite pain and its counterpart: the rain atop a rock. She was all alone, once more – without her child, without her parents, without her lover. No less a miracle than the ones she had seen in the cave, Veni, whose solitude had become her only companion, found her voice and lost her pain on top of a rock in a world far away from home. A distant echo of an ageless song drifted into her tear-stained view of this world:

... in love our hearts are
as red earth and pouring rain:
mingled beyond parting.

7

I WANT TO TALK, COME TO ME. DON'T GO BY HOW sick I look, an old woman my age has the right to look like an ancient tree, but don't assume that just because my body is breaking apart, my mind is too. The lines on my face are like the rings of a tree trunk, each has a tale to tell. Little Veni used to count these lines, lying on her stomach, legs swinging in the air, and with her tiny soft fingers tapping my face she would ask me where I got the five lines on my forehead, where the lines near my eyes were going, what the ones on my lips were all about. She would then touch her unlined face and say, I will take your lines, Aatha, and then people will see that we look the same and the mirrors in our home will be confused. Come, I will tell you a few things the others do not know. How could they? Siddha is not something you learn overnight. You must have it in you and then spend years understanding it, sharing it with those in need, learning by error and experiment, realizing that the flaws of the body are deep, latent movements of the spirit and to heal one, you must heal the other too. You must have heard of me as a midwife but my work and science were more: siddha tells us that *garbhakāla sātviham* involves an understanding of the mother first and foremost for creating a better environment for the unborn child. So, when an expectant mother comes to me, sometimes a mere slip of a girl herself, my foremost duty is to find the girl's inner consciousness, her unique self, as she is drawing upon that inner energy and fire to become the mother that will take care of her young. Unlike lionesses or tigresses to whom nature has given an indomitable will for the protection of their unborn and newly born, human girls are vulnerable, prone to doubt, fear and anxiety. Such a mother is an unwelcome home for the unborn and my duty is to ensure the health of the mother for the health of the child. For many families, the woman is but the vehicle in which a child arrives; this is sheer nonsense. A mother's body *is* the child's body, any wound or disease in the mother directly impacts the child – how can you call such a body a mere vehicle? They are one indivisible unit from birth until death, and siddha knows that the care of the mother is fundamental to ensuring life. So, when those young girls came to my home with their second, fifth, seventh, some even final-month bellies, I looked out for signs of abuse at their home, of fatigue, or bodily shock, all of which a *vaidyar* can see if she keeps her eyes and ears open. Although she was all of eleven or twelve, Veni was always fascinated by siddha and she was a quick learner. While the twins were useful as errand boys, Veni was the one I was slowly, steadily training – she with her one thousand questions and insatiable curiosity about ingredients, and mixing and applying, but also sensitive silence when I was listening to the bellies or massaging the women's feet, forehead or eyes. Veni, this uncanny child, would be my successor, I knew, that is, if her mother and father did not play spoilsport and send her off somewhere either by way of studies or marriage. As she grew up, she learned many aspects of care intuitively, readying her own body for the day she would bring a child into this world, but until then, content to be a part of my siddha, my *sevai*. The young girls who came to me were just children really – *chinna bommai mathiri*, clear-eyed as dolls yet so apprehensive. Pregnancy was a time of revelation for many of them, after a lifetime of living in relative obscurity in their families. Selvi, Sembakam, Agalya, Alamelu, Elimangai, Inbavalli, Radha, Ragini – these girls named after flowers and stars and ancient heroines, who went from being maidens to mothers in a matter of months, all the while learning to suffer aches and pains, fears and anxieties for which they had no preparation or forewarning. For how does one prepare for what one's society thinks is natural to oneself? Young men train and prepare for war; women come ready, it seems, for the war that is pregnancy. Why do you smile – is it not true? Once, you know, a young woman came to me, with her mother-in-law who thought the girl was more tired than is usual for a pregnant girl. I saw, in fact, that the slip of a girl was so fatigued it was hard for her to even hold up her neck which collapsed under the weight of her head, and her arms and feet had grown cold like the earth where you might have buried someone, while her eyes could barely open. I remembered her stomach had been quite large a week or so ago when she had visited me, all signs that there were two, perhaps three, lives inside waiting for the right time. In about a week or so, the stomach seemed unnaturally transformed, distended, and the young mother was slowly leaking blood. Veni rushed some hot towels and warm oil for me and as I applied them to the mother's stomach, I gave her some *kerampola* whose leaf and star-shaped fruit promotes labour. Within minutes, something gave, a pressure seemed released as a lump of flesh, placenta, hair and blood slipped out of her and into Veni's quick-thinking arms, and we realized with shock and sorrow that one of her babies had been stillborn. The woman was semi-conscious and in very little pain, but it became necessary to deliver the other child too, though it seemed reluctant to come out. We wrapped up the dead foetus in a clean, white towel, readying it for a doctor's eye, for what this baby could tell might save the other one. Veni and I prepared the young mother for a long journey – medicines, a hot poultice of assorted herbs for her fluctuating temperature and a warning to not give her any food or water until they met the doctor. I received news in the evening that the young woman had reached the main hospital, three hours away, and two babies – both daughters – were delivered by surgery. My instinct that she was carrying triplets was right but one of the babies died inside the womb and had been in the mother's body for nearly a week, slowly poisoning the insides, until both mother and surviving children fell into danger. The female body is a miracle of nature, in every animal it is so, but perhaps especially among humans, where it lives in a state of great irony, for we worship it and ignore its plight, venerate its utility and neglect its bearer and her health. How do our babies become young women who then become mothers if we do not care for their physical health and mental well-being but expect overnight from them to carry and deliver to us healthy babies? This is surely a kind of malice at work against the woman's body had we also not found ways to make it seem like the most normal thing in the world for young women to take the greatest risk to their lives in the most matter-of-fact of ways and to emerge from the whole experience with their minds and spirits intact. Siddha has no antidote to human cruelty and a vaidyar lives in the sorrowing contradiction of her knowledge that she is nurse and facilitator in a process that has no logic save that of survival, no good but that of the greater over the lesser, the will to procreate always triumphing over the frail, feeble spirit of the woman. But in that process, during that long journey that can be solitary and terrifying for the woman if she is not taught to understand the experience as she is undergoing it, a siddha can come to the woman's aid, can illuminate as best as she can, can lighten, warm, accompany, and this labour is one of love – unceasing, infinite love. It is a sacred duty to birth a woman through pain and carry her to the other side with her newborn, urging her to live, love and flourish. It is heart-work because each woman who came to me became a daughter to me and each child I helped bring into the world became a part of my heart, my siddha. It is possible for human beings, small and ephemeral as our lives are, to yet be a part of something meaningful, something greater than all of us, something ancient and of the future. There is a science and an art to the work of a midwife but so much is also an education – for the mother involved, her family members, and for me, and this education is hard to come by in schools and colleges. This education is from the battleground of life, and it is tied to a deeper knowledge of our place in the world. A young girl expecting to give birth is hardly capable in her mind or her body to fathom the huge responsibility on her slender shoulders, the great promise she holds in herself – a siddha is one who teaches her about the reserves she hides inside. That frail expectant mother is, when at her most vulnerable, no less grand than a king. In the *Purananuru*, it is said:

The path of the crimson sun, its motion, the spheres
around the motion, directions of varying winds,
and all existing vacant spaces without proof –
such matters are well-known to wise folk who can
explain them. Yet such knowledge
is unable to encompass you, since your strength stays concealed
like a stone hidden in the cheek of an elephant.

So is it with the young girls who carry life inside them that childbirth becomes a time of self-discovery, for with the birth of a child, a mother is born, no longer concealed inside a stripling girl. To Veni, I imparted my knowledge and my labour, and she learned that a pregnancy is a war on the woman's body, which she must wage properly and from which she has to be taught to recover. There are no lessons on this in our books and reports, but it is a lesson for life. For my Veni too, there was the joy of having seen as a young child herself the births of so many, even as she also imbibed the eternal sorrow of lost babies. In my view, if you have carried a child in your body for even a day, you are a mother for life. And if you have held a baby in your arms for a minute, you are a mother for life. And if you are a father, then too you are a mother, a caregiver, bound to a life outside yourself forever. Thus it is that we are mothers, all of us, nurturing another life in what way we can, committed to its good, tied forever to its happiness, sharing self and body, spirit and song for as long as we are alive. Our fates are written by forces beyond our will and Veni lost her own child in that vicious attack. Did those men know she was carrying? But had they known, would that have prevented them? Who knows how human will operates? Who knows the limits of ruin man is capable of? Yet, Veni is no stranger to pain – young women go through teeth-shattering pain during pregnancy, quite literally, as so many lose their teeth for lack of calcium in their bodies, or when some women bleed as a part of the pregnancy, a shocking occurrence that the mother learns to normalize. Veni has seen a gamut of shocks and pains to the female body, but did it come to her aid on that savage night – who can say. I taught her everything I could about the female body, its finitudes and infinitudes, but on that black night, blackest of all nights, did any of it come to be of any use to her? Who can say for certain? But they say she hung in there despite the savagery of the attack, they say she gritted so hard that her molars crumbled but the piece of the shirt she wrenched and by which one of the men was later identified remained inside her mouth, they say that although she was battered and kicked and flung around, she protected her spine somehow. They say she took blows to her head and she lost a lot of blood but she dragged herself to dry land and lay there for help, avoiding the oil mill's garbage heap where they left her, and thus staved off infection and sepsis. I knew then that Veni would survive this as one survives an attack by an animal or a grievous accident, she who sacrificed her dreams of being a dancer once understood the nature of her injury – she knew she would make it and she took what steps she could, even in the midst of that great dispossession, to make it to the other side. Siddha refuses to give up life when you can hold it hard, siddha accepts the finality of death but denies ceding one's will to it. Veni has the siddha, a spirit that will never simply give up, not on another in need and not on herself. What are they saying about her? I who am in the last summer of my life, I have the final ignominy of not being there for my child, but I can hope that what I taught her will see her through, clear the bramble and the darkness and take her towards light, the light that shines from inside her, from a place darkness cannot enter or drown – from that place, Veni will climb and siddha will guide her.

8

MURUGA! SIR, MADAM, SIR, WHY YOU DRAGGED ME back from Mathiramalai where I had gone to leave all this shit behind? You think after running about in courts and police stations and how close we had all come to losing everything in life, I would have anything to do with Annathe and his cronies? I am like the burned cat who will not go near the kitchen! I have begun a new life, sir, I swear, no hanky-panky, madam, no crime, sir, proper good man I have become, I promise you, sir, I know nothing about Anna's death. In fact, I thought I had put it all behind me but now the muck is raked up all over again and that accursed woman has bleddy done it. But sir, please listen, sir, I had nothing to do with anything, I promise you. After Annathe and his friends were accused of spoiling Veni, what did that SHO, that monster of a police officer do? He bleddy sent his men after me and they beat me up black and blue. I am just a poor limp, sir, madam, what could I have done to any woman? I cried and begged and told them repeatedly that I had no part in her spoiling but those bleddy police wouldn't stop beating me up. Would they have dared to raise a finger at Annathe or the other men? Murali was their dupe and they all had a go at the cripple. Sir, see, I am crying, these are my tears of torture, madam. They hit me, all of them acting like real bleddy men, thrashing a cripple to death's door. Two of them hit my stomach so many times I lost consciousness, then they threw water at me and when I woke up, they beat me again. Took me several months to recover from the bootkicks and faceslaps, and all the while, the court case dragged on and on. But madam, sir, I will tell you one thing: although I often cursed the day I became a part of Anna's gang, I was also finally glad of the fact. Why? Because I was protected. Because Anna was such a big man, he was virtually untouchable. He got us the best lawyer who told us what to say when-who to, and anyway, we all know this, money talks in our society, *enna* sir, and truth be told, I was glad that for once in my bleddy unlucky existence, I caught a break and I had Annathe in my life and he was going to take care of me. And because he was involved, all of us got off, but those years, with all that uproar in the papers and everything, *yenga appémurugan kapathittan!* I can only say God was watching out for me. But now that this whole ugly business has revived, everything has changed. I don't know how I will bleddy stick to that old story we all said before the police and the court. And with Adhiban Anna gone, who will care for crippled old Murali? Madam, when the pan is too hot, the hand drops it quick – that is my situation. I will be forced to shuffle from one court to the next and whenever some bleddy cop wants to, he will beat the shit out of me. No, no, not you, sir, madam, but that SHO is still there, no, and I am tired of all this running. I will tell you what happened now that Annathe is no longer alive, because with him dead, the others are as good as dead too. Whom can I look to, now that I know a madwoman is on the prowl? Who does Murali have now? *Paithiyam* Murali, *goyyala* Murali! Always the last man to shuffle out of a mess. Always *panni, naai, nattai* – all these animals whose names I had been called all my life, all of them like me – quick to be captured, slow to escape. But I will say it once again: I didn't *do* bleddy anything! Either to that woman or to her family. Try to prove otherwise, I challenge you! No, not challenge *you,* sir, madam, but, but I am saying, I had no part in anything and still they are dragging me here-there and all the while that madwoman is free to do what she likes and who knows she is maybe coming for me next! All this *kundakka mandakka* and I am running for my life again. I paid a great price for simply being Annathe's manservant and what was my role, you ask? I just ran about to get drinks or *vadai* or peanuts for him and his friends when impromptu they decided to drink or to pick up something or drop off or whatever bleddy chores Anna had for his convenience – that's all. Sir, godpromise. Madam, godpromise. Do you think I am such that they would be *friends* with me? I was just a bleddy servant. I hung about because sometimes they shared their foreign liquor and, for a man like me, how could I ever afford stuff like that? It was all fun initially and although Annathe was very insulting and short-tempered, he was sometimes generous to me, leaving me food and drink after he had eaten, and buying me beedi or throwing at me a cigarette pack that I thought was empty but when I shook it, I found it had sometimes one or two smokes in it still. Anna would then laugh aloud and I would join him because though he was a grown-up, he was still a mischievous lad at heart. He would say bleddy this, bleddy that, and somehow my ear loved the sound and I also began to speak his English. Sir, madam, that's how I know English. I picked up things quickly, you see. I was younger than Annathe and, mostly, he treated me like a *sinna thambi,* but, sir, I never ever presumed to be brotherly with him. 'Bleddy rascal!' he would scream and when I ran into the room, he and his friends would explode into howls of laughter. Anna and his friends strung me around to mostly laugh at me, singling out my clothes or footwear or my accent, and I mean how long can one laugh at oneself when the others are actually mocking you? I would laugh with them, but I knew that I was the bleddy fool in all of it. *Goyyala idhu, goyyala adhu*, being called an idiot while also being run around for this and that – that was my main role in the gang, sir, madam, sir. And I knew it. I was their joker and their joke. I did all their errands and stuff but I never was a part of the team – please, madam, put that into your recorder. Thangs, madam. But sir, I was a nobody and what did I care, as long as my food and drink was taken care of and I had a roof over my head? My fear of Annathe always got the better of my needs and that is why on that fateful day, I was hanging about him, sir, but at a distance with an eye and an ear out for when he might holler for me. But *yen viti*, sir, my fate. Can you trick your way out of what is written on your head? Now I know that the catastrophe was fated long ago, when that bleddy girl and her bleddy fool husband were introduced to Annathe. He always had an eye for the ladies especially after his wife died, although even while his wife was alive, Annathe was quite the ladies man, going after what young girl took his fancy. Rich men have that luxury, don't they, sir, and Anna had two houses, one where he put up his family and the second that he used for his 'other' life, his *chinna veedu*. For some reason, he would only let me be around this second place – I called it the cave or the den in my mind because it really was a roomy affair with three rooms along a winding corridor, and all kinds of boxes and stuff stored everywhere in that lair. Only one room with attached bath had a big teak bed and curtains and even an AC for the hot nights. Sir is smiling, I see, yes, Anna's nights were hot for many reasons. Sorry, madam, I am too coarse. Anyway, I was saying, Anna had this other house too and I don't know exactly why but he made sure I was not in contact with his family. I suppose he thought I knew too much and might foolishly spill his secrets. Fat chance of that, sir, madam, I knew enough of that man's wrath to know that one wrong word from me and he would skin me alive. I mean, look what he did to that bleddy girl Veni. I had seen Anna work his magic on women – charm first, power later. Always, in the starting, he was very friendly. They came to him first, you know, sir. What is that? *They* meaning that Veni and her husband. Anna was not of Sittanavasal; he started coming here to help the local school. He did not know the people and the ways of this place, but he did so much good for the school, madam, sir – it always stung him that his parents never had a chance at education and then he dropped out in some lower division also, but that did not stop him and he was quite the patron, getting benches, chairs, blackboards, paying for the school's annual picnic, and providing all kinds of support during the heavy rain also. Soon he began to have sway over the hiring of staff too, especially the teachers. But it was a bleddy racket, I tell you, sir – worth several thousand rupees for each job. He liked recommending young women who, he claimed, were very motherly. In their childhood, all children need a mother-like figure in school too, Anna used to say. Of course, the mother-like figures he got were *battil mathri*, what we bottle-lovers locally call *figaru*. You smile, sir, but these are all fun things – harmless, madam, *summa*. That bleddy old principal, he is the one who introduced all of them to each other. Anna said he would get the husband a job there, and I don't know what strings he pulled or whom he called up, but the school needed a teacher for mathematics and Veni's man came right at the time. Bleddy fucking fate, right? He, that husband of hers, he was a pukka *yidiot* but *she,* she was a *kili* – from the starting, I knew Anna had a vibration for that bird. He liked to ogle girls with long hair especially, this was a thing with him, and she was a real figure, what we call a *gujili*.

She wasn't a beauty with like, you know, cinema glamour, but there was something about her that caught your bleddy eye – she walked like she didn't really care and there was always a kind of – I don't know, sir, something about her, I don't know what to say, madam, I am not good at these words – she made it seem like she was superior to us all. Most women tended to get Anna's ways very quickly and I've seen two responses only: either the woman surrenders to his power and *macho* or they get that he has designs on them and start to avoid him or otherwise fear him. But Veni was different, sir, madam – she behaved as if she didn't at all get what Anna wanted from her or if she did get it, like it didn't matter to her. She was so indifferent that Anna was himself baffled. When they met at school or outside the temple, she would barely acknowledge his existence and if her husband was around, she would drift off to some local flower-seller or store while Anna had to make small talk with the husband whom he absolutely despised. What could Anna do when she was like this? He couldn't bleddy figure her out, he said. One particular incident always stayed a sore point with him. It was a small thing really, sir, but big men's reputations are such that even small things take on big size, no. And it stayed in my mind. Once Anna had been invited to a trophy ceremony at the school. Every year, he along with some town bigwigs came to give one, two trophy to well-performing students. This time, instead of a trophy for the first rankholder, the gift was one of those round things on a stand, you know – the one with drawings of the whole world? Anyway, there is one English word for it, and Anna just was not able to speak it. Gobbil or glubb or something, I can't remember now. Initially, we were all a little quiet as Anna stammered through the tricky word on the microphone, but soon, after one or two attempts, there was a giggle among the students sitting in the front row and, slowly, everyone started laughing. But most of all, Veni found the whole thing hilarious and standing in one corner with all the other female teachers, she began giggling, hiding her face behind her saree, but the more she suppressed her laugh, the more the other women caught on, and Anna turned red in the face and nearly threw the ball at the panic-stricken child who had come up on stage to receive the glub or whatever. Although Annathe stayed for the whole function, I could see his whole mien was changed after that incident and he was only pretending to complete the formalities. Once the programme was over, he did not stay back for the usual coquetry with the lady teachers, and marching to the driver, he took the car's keys. Then he got into the driving seat of his white Ambassador and asking me to sit next to him, drove off. Sir, madam, I still remember the incident. I had carried into the car all the flowers and bleddy garlands they had put on him but about ten minutes into our drive, he stopped the car and asked me to throw everything out. We drove in silence after that but his hands on the steering wheel were tight and draining of blood and I was so bleddy afraid that he would crash us into some tree or rock that I clenched my mouth and looked outside the window throughout the journey. Anger, they say, no, sir, madam, anger is more destructive than the sword, and the anger of a great man is the most terrifying thing of all. That night, we went to his other house, where Anna spent time with one of his women and he was especially rough on her. As I sat smoking my beedi outside in the humid dark, I could hear faint cries and screams, although then I couldn't tell if they were of pleasure or pain. When I woke up around 5 a.m., there was no sign of the girl, and Anna was asleep on the bed naked, covered only by a bedsheet, and there were several half-burnt and crushed cigarettes about, knocked-over glasses, half-spilled liquor bottles, and clothes strewn everywhere in the room. I found the girl's undergarments near the bed but there was no sign of her saree or blouse, and I guessed that she must have left in a hurry. When Annathe woke up, he was still angry, sore from a headache, he said, and the whole day, I scampered around, answering to his every need, and yet he threw things about and yelled at me for being bleddy slow. That was it – the one bleddy incident that I think just stayed like a hot coal in his chest, smoking him up from the inside, and any mention of that day or of Veni after that incident would raise his ire. He could get furious at the drop of a hat, and like an elephant, he remembered slights and offences for a long time. His anger was frightening, and I was never sure when he might strike me dead. And that is the truth, sir, madam, I was deathly afraid of him. And after that school incident, I think he took to his heart Veni's mocking laughter and I suppose, he just waited for the right time to pay back. His cronies, especially that scoundrel Samuel, that guy had a special penchant to really rile up Anna. You are drooling today, *jollu vidathingé, Anna*, he mocked the next time they all met up, indirectly referring to Veni's laughter and Anna's stammering fiasco trying to speak English. Samuel then began speaking of Veni and her husband in jest, and I heard him but cowered away because he did not really know Annathe's volcanic anger like I did. That day, however, Anna remained smiling like a saint. *Avan oru jujubi, da*, Anna said, insulting the husband and then, they all laughed because it's easy to snigger at the small fry of the world. On such days, I too would join in the laughter but of course, you think I don't know that they called me jujubi behind my back too? And what is *she*, Samuel needled, his beady brown eyes glowing with spite. *Aval oru semmakattai, da!* And they roared with mirth because Anna was being dandy with words, calling Veni both a figaru and a log of wood, inert, frigid. But as he downed his foreign liquor, I could see Anna's whole face was tight, his jaw clenched as if he was seething inside and something about his laugh drove a chill into my heart, sir. Like a beast in *must*, he was most dangerous when he was calm and quiet and seemingly playful. I knew then some *galatta* was coming, some impending calamity. And sure as hell, *mayire!* (*Ayyo*, sorry, madam! Forgive me!) I was saying, when that Samuel called Annathe to the old mill where they all sometimes got together if good local liquor was available, who knew how it would all swell up, like the Kaveri in spate? It all began with them bleddy men calling each other names. Madam, you have to forgive what I am going to say now. Sorry, sir, but this is what happened, and I want to tell everything to your recorder. You put your hands on your ears, madam. Shall I continue, sir? So, I was saying that when they got at the old mill, the men started name-calling. *Poda pundai nakki*, yelled Samuel at Vengattu because he was becoming attached to a local *owsari*, a Kannada whore he had picked up but who, I have to admit, was a sweet girl in her own way. Whenever I dropped Anna's packets at her place – what? packets of stuff, I don't know what. How would I know, sir? I was just carrying from one place to next. That woman's job was to pass packets on to two truck-drivers who came to her, but she was a nice girl, you know, sir, she would make me sweet freshlime when I made the delivery. Anyway, so Vengattu got hot under his collar – I mean, we all knew he loved the girl but what could he do, a whore never quits until her cunt cools down and this one was so bleddy young, she had just begun. So, he was always a little off in his head, Vengattu, about his love for a whore and with the *sarakku* flowing through his veins, more full of liquor than blood, he was ready to fly off the handle when Samuel called him a cunt-licker. Samuel was like that, sir, very cheap. But then Annathe, I don't know if he was just horny that evening or if he was actually drunk, we were all well past tipsy for sure, even me, because to be honest, our local sarakku is much kinder on my stomach – I have gas problems, you see – and I was slyly guzzling a glass here, and one there, all the while making sure the *periya paruppu,* them big shots were all happily plied with country liquor. I'll give that guy Kannan one thing – he could get the best local stuff, he had a great network and he could, at the snap of a bleddy finger, manage to put together an evening in no time. So, there we were, sir: Anna, Samuel, Vengattu, Kannan and me – by the old mill, spending our men's evening together, the sun having dropped low and the sky almost golden, I remember very well, sir. I was actually looking through my half-filled glass into the sunlight when I first saw Veni from afar. Her yellow sari tucked behind her, she was bending low near some trees where the women sometimes come to pick mushrooms. I would recognize that thick braid of hers anywhere but with my eyes somewhat swimming with liquor and the evening sky so bleddy romantic and all that talk about Vengattu's whore, I don't know what came over me, but I ran back to Anna, all pleased and said, *'Anna! Anna! Veni vandrikka!'* As soon as the bleddy words were out of my mouth, I could have slapped my face a dozen times because Anna froze and Samuel and Vengattu looked at each other, and my bleddyfool heart began thudding loudly inside my chest. For a moment, there was thunder in my ears and when Anna slapped my head, twice, because I hadn't heard him the first time, I heard him ask me in a low, almost gentle voice, *'engé, da?'* I pointed mutely towards the tall *iluppai maram*, and from our vantage we could, when we tried, see snatches of yellow move around and behind the tree-trunk. Anna downed his glass in one gulp and his three friends did the same. What was I waiting for? I also did the same. My fear and excitement, sir, a strange heady brew was driving me mad although everything in my head was telling me to scream loudly and say to the men, *don't go!* And to Veni, *go! run!* One scream could have shattered the quiet of the place, could have warned her off, but no voice came out of my bleddy throat, and the men got up silently, like dogs to a whistle that no human ear can hear. They slipped off their chappals and like a pride of lions stalking their prey, they fanned out to reach her from different directions. Sir, madam, sir, I can't forget that evening. Annathe was the first to head forth, followed by Samuel, then Kannan, and then Vengattu, and I was the last, and as usual, I was barely able to keep up, my bleddy limp making sure I was the laggard in any group. There was a herd of buffaloes splashing in the pond around which the mill's waste was piled. A sickening stink came from the place, but the mill had been shut for months and the last bits of foul refuse continued to foam and leach into the water. I remember this because mushrooms grew in plenty hereabouts, which was the reason Veni came there that evening of all bleddy evenings. I saw that Kannan had pulled up his lungi to cover his nose but his stride had not broken. When the men first reached Veni, I hadn't yet made it to the group. But I could hear their voices through all the bush, Veni's feminine voice the least audible, while the men's gruff words were much easier to get. 'You love mushrooms? You should ... told us ... packets and packets are traded ... sure to get ... Yellow suits your dusky ... husband? ... We all like you a lot, Veni. Do you like us?' I swear, sir, I couldn't hear much else. Snatches of their banter became clear as I limped closer. '*Dei, Murali, paar ra!*' Anna barked suddenly, using my given name rather than the customary goyyala and instantly I understood he meant for me to keep watch. I stopped and looked around. Like a knife goes clean through a *pusani*, her screams cut open the air, as Samuel and Kannan grabbed Veni tightly in their powerful arms. She began to flail like a fish fighting against the angler when Annathe grabbed her hair, twisting it until she screamed in pain, and then he gave her a slap that sounded like a firecracker had gone off. She was still for a minute, wilting in the arms of the men, but soon she rallied and began to fight back once again, and this time, Anna's roar brought Vengattu into the party, who had so far been standing frozen and then that bleddy Vengattu rushed to cover her mouth. In sheer terror, I tell you, sir, madam, I whipped my head looking around the overgrowth and the abandoned mill, my heart pounding a bleddy din in my ears, worried beyond all limits of reason that someone would hear us, see us, and we would all be caught. Annathe had no such fears and he moved like a seasoned actor, the kind we seen so often, sir, in the stage dramas that came to Pudukottai. He looked like one such actor himself, so sure he seemed, sir, as he gave duties to each of the men. All of a sudden, Vengattu screamed like a bleddy madman and started waving a hand in the air and I saw that Veni had bit him hard on his palm, which was oozing blood. In anger and pain, Vengattu gave it to her, twice, thrice, all the while wincing in his own agony. Veni crumpled and fell, and at that moment, Annathe pushed me away further from them and ordered me to keep a lookout. I understood that he did not want me near them or the girl. And my heart, sir, madam, was booming in my ears, I was glad to go. After I moved out, everything was a blur of time for me. I looked away from all of them but I suppose I could imagine from the dull thuds and slaps what was going on. I thought I heard the sounds of bone cracking, but in the overgrowth, it was hard to separate natural sounds from the din the men were making. Today, if you ask me, I don't know what I heard really – *yenna*, sir, believe me, the sounds were so mixed. It was a din, at least to my ears, and yet no one, bleddy no one came towards the mill and I could hear or see nobody from the large weeds I was crouching behind. It felt like several hours but it must have been only minutes as I squatted on my haunches and twisted left right left right, trying to sight any movement or hear any sound that might make the men stop. I had to balance myself using my hands, and in that strange position, so hard with my left leg congenitally shorter than the right, I felt like a monkey guarding the forest in Lanka. And then, the dull screams died down and after a while, I could only hear long gasps or sudden short ones, without knowing who was making those sounds. Sunlight peeked through the bushes all around and evening was quick to set in. I was glad for the dark, sir, madam, to be honest, because then I couldn't see the faces of the men any more, only silhouettes moving, standing, crouching. In the lowering light, I thought I saw a sneer on the face of Samuel once and suddenly it struck me, how bleddy ugly that man was, inside and out. If I was a woman, I could never be attracted to such a face. Kannan is a swarthy man, with a back built like a buffalo's, very useful for moving sacks of grain or picking up large furniture. When he moved towards Veni, I wondered briefly how his massive frame must crush her small body. Only one lean, lanky figure stood apart watching – I recognized it as Vengattu's. I didn't know how much longer it would all take but my hands were trembling a little, or maybe a lot, I don't remember. Vengattu was holding his palm high, now wrapped up in a torn shirt, trying to stem the flow of blood with the other. He seemed to not want to go to Veni and when Anna pushed him towards her, he just kicked her, I think. After that ... madam, sir, I couldn't see very clearly by that point, I couldn't *really* see, sir, but I don't think, yeah, I don't think he did anything else. Anyway, when Vengattu stopped, I saw Annathe walk over, and he raised his right leg once near her middle. I looked away then and suddenly, I was so bleddy tired, my calves ached, my chest was hurting, and there were gnats all around – what the hell was I doing there anyway, I was so angry at myself, at my bleddy fucking life that had landed me into that moment! When at last we left the damned place, there was no sound coming out of her. To be honest, sir, I don't know what I thought then – maybe that she was finally, luckily, dead. I mean, madam, let's admit it, that would have been best for her and all concerned. But as it turned out, she wasn't, right? There was a lot of life still in her and the whole thing just blew up on us. Since that day, my heart beats in terror, sir, I tell you, terror – I don't know what calamity will next fall on me, I don't know when some police jeep will stop outside my door, when someone will put a bag over my head and take me godknowswhere, I've lived constantly in fear, sir. Until the court set all of us free, there was not a night I slept in calm, sir, madam. Even when Anna and the others were laughing, I was terrified of the smallest sound like one fears being hit by a bat in the dark night. Those were difficult days and nights, sir, and I thought I had finally put it all behind me when I started life again in Mathiramalai, far away from all this *galatta*. But now see what this Veni has done. She had all my goodwill and pity, but this bleddy revenge on Annathe is too much. They say his family cremated his body with a coconut filled with ghee where his head should have been. *Enna*, sir, does one get *moksham* this way? Madam, where is the police and justice for Anna? And now they are all saying she has bleddy disappeared? Ayyo, sir! She is lying low and she is coming for the rest of us. I am telling the bleddy police this and they are not listening to me. Vengattu has run off with his whore. Samuel and Kannan have powerful friends so I am sure they are not feeling any fear. I am the only one who is without a bleddy benefactor now that my Annathe is gone – and between madness and fear, I don't know what I will be doing, who I will be going to, sir, madam! Ayyo, Muruga, damn that bleddy woman to hell!

9

MY BROTHER AND I WERE ALWAYS BUSY WITH CRICKET matches – there were days when we played for hours, six, eight, ten hours, not caring about the time or hunger. There was that perfect cover drive or a catch taken just microseconds before the ball plummeted to the ground, or the diving, running, throwing, screaming, jumping, handshaking, back-thumping – a whole sequence of intensities, one after the other, so that when you left the field and returned home to food, family, sleep, the pulse of everything dropped and neither of us could be still or sleep in anticipation of the next day. This wildness was so all-consuming we hardly noticed our sister, and you could say this was selfishness, our self-absorption, but we knew no different, you know, we were told no different, and now I have no way of knowing anything else in this life other than this, this sport, which has itself turned into a battlefield for me, for us, because we are both fighting inside it and lying dead on the side. No, no, cricket was all-consuming but we were not serious: neither of us dreamed of playing for money or for fame; to play was everything. How long could this bubble have survived? Appa worked hard for us and Amma took care of home. What need did we have for contributing, my brother and I, *thambi*, always *thambi*, to Akka, elder sister, who called us *periya thambi* – I a whole seven minutes older – and Chinna *thambi* – he, hustling behind, seven minutes too late – in a kind of mock-bird-like sound, an in-joke of names we paraded before extended family. In private, we called each other *pannri*, *erumai* and *kakkai*, a whole range of animal names we combined to create fantastical creatures; the more fantastical they were, the more creative the jibe. But we missed so much, Chinna and I. We missed seeing Akka growing up, and I now wonder, did our parents also miss them? Did they miss all those years when we grew up together into different creatures, no longer the little cells, split halfway between Amma and Appa, not quite persons but mere halflings, only to be born into new wholes, each *one*, *not* the other, but my brother and I, linked in birth by a mysterious unity, sharing space and knowing no other way of life but his spine against mine, his thumb inside my mouth, bubbles from my nose mingling with his, while we lay supine inside Amma. Is this how we came because I look at my brother now, in the absence of my sister, and I can only see half his head and when I look closely into his eyes, with horror, I see the reflection of my face and I am half a head too, and we are both halflings once more. I suppose, you could ask your questions and, in all honesty, we would have to say, we only *knew* of the other brother, as a head knows the leg, and there was no time or room to know our other self-body, Akka, and we saw her but did not *see* her, so that when we became men, in moustaches and light beards and broken voices, each brother knew the other man but we barely knew Akka as woman, as an entity of her own. We recognized her, of course, in play, in jest, as a sharer of our home, but we boys, we learned to leave home early, for a life of play so obsessive that *that* was life and home was a mere shelter for the night, a lull before the real thing and the real thing always was the company of other boys, the brotherhood of play, the competition of it, the all-consuming physicality of sport. I can barely recall tranquil moments of my childhood, moments of quiet, or silence, apart from sleep, and how well we slept, assured of our place in the order of things, safe, accepted, so that we missed seeing Akka running in the bushes after the chameleons or climbing the terrace to see the stars at night, hiding her menstrual rags after washing and drying them, or wearing kohl in her limpid eyes, or threading flowers for her long hair. We missed *seeing* her for so long that we don't know now who has left us: has she gone away or disappeared, as you say, now, or was she never there, to begin with? But wait, I forget something – Chinna, *da*, you remember walking with Akka to her dance classes? Watching her from the window and the other girls, all moving rhythmically, but Akka also looking at us peering in, and then winking big so that we giggled and she smiled and so did some of the other girls, and guru-amma getting angry and hitting her *taalam* once, twice, thrice, breaking rhythm and the girls, all jumping in disarray, all unison gone, and us holding the bars of the window tight and shaking like little monkeys until driven away. What happened to those two boys? I do not know why but suddenly that memory came to me. Maybe it is the sight of her empty room and its bare window, the bars holding in her memories and her absence. Childhood was such an absorptive time that I wonder whether our youth has been merely an extension of it – how were we to learn to remove ourselves from the centre of this world we inhabited and look at another person – our Akka – as inhabiting the same world albeit at a different point of existence from us? If Chinna had been taken away from me, I would have collapsed as if a saw had halved me, but why was I not drawn to Akka in the same way? She whom Appa took on private sojourns down the hills and up the rock temple, whom Amma and Aatha adored, spending hours caring for her hair, perhaps Chinna and I carved our own world for the reason that we were so *outside* the realm of our family's immediate preoccupations. Did we know that around Akka our domestic world ran and did we think we orbited elsewhere? I do not know how exactly I learned to differentiate between the happenings in my home and those of my companions – maybe Chinna does but now we will never know. I recall how in other homes, the boys we played with had the run of the place while their sisters skulked in corners, receiving the second-best pieces of fish or leftovers of sweetmeats after the men and boys of the house had eaten. When Chinna and I visited a friend's home, we were also extended the same extra love and care, while shy sisters would eye us from behind doors or windows as we ate heartily and mothers and grandmothers and aunts showered us with love and praise for things we did not do. In our home, Chinna and I were like stray cats – we came and left, there was always food to be had, Amma and Aatha loved us but were so busy during the day that we ran after them asking for little things while they shooed us off and then we bounced off to their doughty assistant, Akka, who would make time for us and chase us about even as she satisfied our little wants and needs. Ours was an unusual family and we grew up seeing so many pregnant women, while Chinna and I, the only boys in the house, for Appa was away at work, we ran between the legs of giant, tottering women as they came looking for medicine, advice, water, food, company. Aatha and Akka took care of these women, flitting from one to the other, the house drowned in a cacophony of sighs and cries and litanies of pains and aches, as Chinna and I bounced like airy footballs from one woman's stomach to another, two little balloons aimlessly bobbing, getting in everyone's way, until Amma yelled at us to get out, go, play. And as we ran about, we heard so many stories, of young girls who didn't want their babies, of women apprehensive that the two or three hungry devils inside their belly would eat all their organs, of frantic mothers bringing their pregnant daughters because they bled suddenly, and Chinna and I – *enna da,* do you remember? – we learned of women's bodies and children's bodies so early and we thought, how utterly magical that young girls like Akka could balloon up one day and pouf out a little boy or little girl who would then bobble around with its unstable head on a tiny neck and be passed from arm to arm, all the while, the bystanding mothers cooing at the tiny thing in love and joy and welcome. Those were the days before play took over our lives and I remember running around, above, beneath the curtains and bedsheets that were hung all about the house for the women to feel private within, while some lay down on the floor, others were collapsed on chairs or stools, like huge whales after a big meal, and Chinna and I running about with steel tumblers full of ice-cold water while Akka scampered about with wet towels and Aatha put her ears to the whale bellies and spoke in a tongue we didn't know. When she heard an answer, she smiled and rewarded the woman with ice water and a kiss on her forehead. How much I yearned then to get Aatha to kiss me but she was so busy and when she had time, she only looked at Akka, so that Chinna and me, we wondered how Amma had brought us into the world, for maybe Aatha had not kissed Amma's forehead or blown bubbles into her belly-button where we may have received her messages, and so when we came out, Aatha barely knew Chinna and me and the two of us were always belated, catching up, but never reaching. And now, damned to be without Akka, our fragile home is shattered, as Aatha lies on her cot like a wingless bird in its last hour, Appa leaving and coming into the house with his head bowed, his eyes afraid to meet ours – what do our eyes say to him, I wonder – and Chinna and I, incapable of being inside, we escape during the day and the evenings to other parts of town; only now I must guard my Chinna as I neglected to guard Akka. Our evenings, bare of the life we had when we played and swam and ate wherever, attended school on some days and played truant on others, Chinna and I both in the wrong classroom, having failed a few times, but happy to be in a cricket team, playing our hearts out, throwing our lives for a high, curving catch, or fighting with the opponent team as if our honour depended on it. Was it so wrong, I now think, to have lived our lives like two boys, feckless, innocent, carefree? Why was it so wrong? Did we not deserve our life, our fragile calm? Who ... when ... I forget now what I was going to say. I forget so many details but some things I remember vividly – the taste of the cricket ball, the smell of our shirts drenched in sweat and dust, the touch of cotton in my home ... these seem like they are not memories, but snatches from a film I saw in some other life. And everything changed overnight the day Akka was attacked and left for dead. When Chinna and I ran from the field towards the old mill, little did we realize how utterly our lives were going to change. Chinna was always more fleet than me, so he ran ahead, while I trailed behind, the same thought in both our heads: did that boy say Akka was *dead*? By the time we got there, a crowd had already formed and we had to push past many. Chinna roughly shoved aside a few men who hit him back with anger, not knowing why or who, while I screamed '*Akka! Akka! Akka! Akka!*'. Hearing me, Chinna screamed too, and we were let go. And when we fell to our knees next to the body, it was Akka indeed in blood everywhere, her blouse torn open, a bloody stone lying next to her, gurgling from her mouth, her breath still coming in hoarse gasps, and we heard her try to say something but it sounded like *gluglugluggglug*. Chinna roared in pain and took off his lungi, flinging it over Akka's body, jolting a bunch of others, shocked into inaction thus far, to grab a cotton sheet from somewhere and cover Akka and scream 'doctor, doctor'. The next thing I remember is rushing to the town hospital, a blur of activity, nurses scurrying about, the resident doctor overwhelmed by Akka's state and by the commotion and pressure of it all. The next few days oscillated between public scrutiny, police interrogation, media frenzy, and nights of total silence and a paralysing inertia. When Chinna heard that Adhiban and his friends were involved, without a word, he grabbed an aruval and went out of the house, the garden sickle held tight in his unsteady hand. Appa was catatonic and a frantic Amma begged me to go after him and bring him back. I did but as ever, Chinna was agile, and he jumped over people's yards and roads to head towards the town bar where men congregated in the evenings. It was a local haunt for Adhiban when he came visiting but that night, he was nowhere to be seen and neither were his cronies. Chinna lurched about in the night, waving the aruval, screaming at the other customers, some sympathetically drawing him away, which is how I found him, raving like an animal, frothing from his mouth, tears streaming down his face as he yelled obscenities and threats at his vanished foes. He was like the wild, raging bull the ancient poets sang of, driven to the very edge of reason, a shred away from madness, and that night, for the first time ever in our lives, I feared Chinna. I feared his anger and I feared what it would do to me and to him and I cursed Akka for having been born. I cursed my sister. My shame, the scalding shame of it all! You should have seen him that night,

> *Like a bull with multitudes of spots that resemble*
> *Inthiran with a thousand eyes ...*
> *Like that crimson bull who gores again and again ...*
> *Like that white bull that leaps high*
> *with the man hanging desperately by his neck ...*

As I watched him, restrained by people while he screamed profanities, I quivered in my heart and terror shook me for I feared what was to come to Akka, to all of us. Somehow, we managed to quiet him but he was not be denied for long and, in a few days, as the furore began to subside somewhat, while Akka was still hanging between life and death in the hospital, now across town, a bigger affair, more facilities, more doctors, Chinna began to rouse a small army of our friends to look for some of the men Akka had named during her many bouts of sinking consciousness. The first to be caught was that lowlife called Murali, a limp, as they say, but when he was caught, he was barely coherent, someone having got to him before Chinna did and he was banged up beyond recognition. In time, we learned that Murali was the lookout but he himself did not participate, leaving the heinous work to his four bosses, the overlord of whom was Senganoor Adhiban. You write that name down, since you are wondering where his head is. You write it down properly this time with the date and year correct, okay? But what is time to the likes of you? So many months and years passed since we cried ourselves hoarse at our sister's plight, at the hardheartedness of the police and the judges, and what was the point of our tears? What came of it all anyway? Those men, all of them, were let free to roam in arrogance and hate, while my elders and family members cowered in fear of reprisals. The freedom of those men set a time bomb upon my family, who would set it off, when, it was all foretold but to live under the shadow of death is no life. Time has frozen since, and all of us caught in its grip, its chokehold on each of our necks so visible to anyone who cares to look into our faces, black marks just like those on Akka's neck where the men pinned her down, cutting off her breath, driving her to madness and the edge of consciousness from which place, who knows what she felt, who can say what went through her mind. Ask Chinna what happened next, but you will not receive an answer, you know why? Because those men returned two years after their acquittal, confident that the scandal had died, confident of the police and the politicians that had stacked up together in their favour and set them free, and on a day like today, two months ago, on a day that should have been perfectly ordinary, Chinna found them near the old grounds, enjoying a laugh, drinking to old times, and he launched himself upon them. But he was one and they were many: with their paid hands, they overpowered him, and Adhiban punched his head so badly my brother never recovered from the concussions, lost his hearing in one ear and vision in one eye, and then to prove what they could do to Akka, they cut out his tongue. So, Chinna sits here, my halfling, silent as stone, his bloodless mouth a cave from which no sound comes other than the echoes of words he wishes to scream, grunts and rumbles of a fire that burns somewhere deep within him and me, scorching our insides as it did our Akka's and turning our world ashen forever. You came looking for Akka, no? But meet my twin brother first. Chinna, *enge da?* Remember, brother:

Bulls dig out the intestines of men with their decorated horns.
Eagles fly high carrying the intestines that slip
from their beaks, falling upon tree branches, looking
Like flower garlands dangling on the banyan and katampam trees
as offerings.

Enna, sir, why do you grow pale? Is it because Chinna wears Akka's saree and tonguelessly smiles at you? Akka has flown but Chinna walks as she used to around town, you can see him skipping over rocks, murmuring '*kuṟiñci, mullai, marutam*' at the hidden stars of the day, welcoming the little *pāpa* she was bringing for her luckless brothers as a gift. You will see him walking all day long in his Akka's clothes, gathering fruits and berries, talking soundlessly to plants and the smallest of beings. He goes around looking for four beasts, the four beasts Akka sought and never found. She had things to ask of them, she said to us, so now Chinna does what she cannot – he goes looking in her place. Don't you, *da*? *Ayyo, paittiyom*. Come, my halfwit brother, come close, Chinna. Sit.

10

Crime Details Report

Case File of Investigating Officer: AP Peter, Assistar Commissioner of Police

FIR No. or Crime number, Police Station, section of law and the place of occurrence, date	The name of the person who shows the place of occurrence	The modus operandi adopted in this case by the accused, if applicable	Particulars of victims
KJ/23/412/MO PK 239 Sittanavasal, 29/08/2002	Natarajan (alias Raja)	Decapitation by sickle, aruval; Head and weapon missing	Senganoor Adhiban

Motive, if known	Details of properties stolen / involved	Date & time of visit to the spot	Description of the place of occurrence, (Prominent landmarks to be mentioned)	SHO/IO report
Possible case of revenge; personal enmity cannot be ruled out	No money involved; Head of deceased missing	Thursday 29 Aug. 2002; 7 pm approx.	Main market junction; outside Tirupathi Bar-cum-Restaurant	IO Asha P. Peter report; please see below

Crime Details Report of Investigating Officer: ACP Asha Puduppari Peter

Police has spoken with concerned relatives of both accused and deceased. All reports have been filed under separate heads. Enclosed is Crime Details Report.

On 29 August 2002, at approximately 6:45 pm, one Natarajan, a local, informed police of a dead body outside Tirupathi Bar-cum-Restaurant and took first officers to spot at 7 p.m. approx. On scene, officers found a decapitated body, identified by Natarajan and others to be that of Senganoor Adhiban. Police found wallet containing Voter ID Card of Senganoor Adhiban, money (total: Rs. 760), and bill-cum-receipt of food and drinks from Tirupathi Bar-cum-Restaurant. Officers immediately cordoned area and called for back-up. Weapon used appears to be a local garden knife or sickle, an aruval with bent blade. Forensic report of neck wound will confirm type of weapon used.

Adhiban's body was found next to car (white Ambassador TN0A4391). No other victims have been found or reported. No witnesses to the homicide have come forward.

Crime seems, prima facie, to be one of passion. Witnesses have attested to seeing a woman with short hair, walking in saree, holding what allegedly looked like a head by its hair in her right fist. Witnesses claim the woman was walking towards the temple on top of the Sittanavasal rocks. Some 600 metres from said temple, remains of human hair have been found. Hair looks, prima facie, of a woman and was burned using matchsticks. Partially burned remains of clothing which appear to be remnants of saree and blouse and empty matchboxes were also found in the charred residue and have been sent for forensic analysis. Witnesses who claim to have seen a figure walk in the fading light of evening cannot confirm identity of person.

Prime accused is one K. Sriveni. It may be noted that four years ago, in 1998, the accused had filed charges of gangrape and sexual assault against deceased Adhiban and four others. In 2000, Hon'ble High Court acquitted all accused (Adhiban included) for lack of clear evidence corroborating K. Sriveni's allegations.

Witnesses have alleged that seven weeks ago, Adhiban and some men allegedly attacked K. Sankar, alias Chinna, younger brother of K. Sriveni, causing grievous body harm to Sankar, which included multiple concussions to the head, breakage of nose, partial loss of vision and cutting out of tongue. FIR was filed on 12 July 2002 in connection with the attack and investigation is pending.

A rough sketch of crime scene is enclosed with report.

BY THE TIME ASHA PETER PUT HER SIGNATURE ON the Crime Details Report, it was nearly midnight. The nightsky teemed with stars. She was here because the deceased was a local politician and the manner of his death had sensationalized an old rape case, compelling the ministry to send a proper IPS officer for investigation. It was the new century and the clamour from NGOs and local media was spreading fast. If she messed it up, Crime Branch was bound to be called in; so, there was a lot of pressure on her to tie up loose ends. As ACP, Asha was an anomaly in the force. Her quiet, introspective demeanour and interest in criminal psychology fit the profile of an academic or writer better and a natural talent for communication made her the department's go-to person for training incoming recruits. Now, after nearly a decade in service, Asha had carved a name for handling 'sensitive' cases involving sexual abuse or gender-based violence, the kind that threatened to blow up like a political powder keg if quick results were not furnished. So, there she was, brought in to Pudukottai Central Zone for the Adhiban beheading case, a mountain of evidence staring at her on the dining table, thick files to wade through, several spools of tape to be heard, and all the while, the pressure was building on her to find a missing woman. But right now, she had to think through a throbbing migraine, a result of the loudspeakers in her area blaring songs all night. Particularly ear-rending was a song where the beloved was being courted by a tireless beau who refused to take no for an answer and wooed her by comparing the girl to fish, peacocks, even, for some unfathomable reason, Asha noted in some alarm, to a closed drum. When she couldn't take it anymore and visions of firing her service pistol in the air invaded her oppressed brain, she called the station to send a *havildar* to speak to the celebrating party. Twenty minutes after the call, blessed silence reigned. Pulling rank was not something she liked to do but sometimes exceptions had to be made.

This new case was also exceptional, very different from the kind Asha usually tackled. Here, the who, when, where, how and even the why of the crime seemed clear. She had to write 'prima facie' on her report, especially since the final forensics, medical and some other case reports were still awaited, but, in fact, there did not seem to be much apart from what was obvious. The only catch was that the accused had vanished from the face of the earth! For days now, the police had been searching for the woman and the head of the decapitated man. Some thirty personnel were combing the area but there seemed to be no trace of her. A sniffer dog had led them to the point where they found burned hair along with charred remains of clothing. From that point, who helped her escape, where to, and how, were all a mystery. It was as if the earth had swallowed her up! The possibility that someone helped her get away and escape to some city or out-of-state location could not be ruled out and Asha had already set in motion the missing-persons protocol. In the meantime, the police interviewed family members and close friends of the accused. All of them pointed to the accused's gangrape and sexual violation by the deceased four years ago as the chief cause for this crime and there seemed to be broad consensus that the attack on the younger brother two months ago was the catalytic event. But that said, the accused had behaved in unpredictable and unforeseeable ways, and Asha now wondered if there was more to this case than what met the eye.

The deceased, Senganoor Adhiban, was a local bigwig who liked to interfere. He had made the situation in Mullur much worse by conniving with upper-caste Hindus to bar the entry of Dalits into the great two-hundred-year-old temple for which Mullur was known far and wide. The resulting clash between communities led to the deaths of two Dalit men and injury to several others. The place was still on boil. What was his connection with Sittanavasal? With its Jaina caves and Hindu temple, Sittanavasal was a place of ancient syncretism and coexistence among communities. Was he trying to foment trouble here or make a buck by black-marketing relics of the monastery or the temple? Asha had read reports of the Archaeological Survey of India investigating the possibility that the Jaina monastery was tied to a complex of caves, as yet undiscovered, which might contain evidence of an old, historical community in the hoary past. If that were true, then the likes of Adhiban would certainly come sniffing. She scanned the victim sheet on Adhiban: he was a widower, his wife having died in childbirth, and his only son lived with the extended family in Surulimalai. He had two extortion charges and two cases of land grab and forceful eviction against him, all ongoing. The gangrape and assault case was by far the most serious crime he had been charged with but one in which he had been acquitted. But Adhiban was also a community man and a patron of the local school, football ground, and the communal fisheries. He had integrated himself really well and had a secure circle of friends in high places. After almost ten years in the police, Asha was unsurprised that there was a sexual angle to his excesses, but she wondered about the rape and attack on Sriveni: what was it motivated by? And if this homicide was a crime of passion, as they called it in police parlance, then it seemed clear to her that revenge was Sriveni's motive.

The question of motive was always prickly, Asha knew: what motivates a man to attack a woman and rape her? Is it lust, a power trip, or the urge to be cruel without fear of punishment? But what kind of punishment will *prevent* crimes against women? As a woman herself, Asha had a tendency to sympathize with women – in her line of work, more often than not, when women claimed to be victims, they were. The occasional instance of a woman perpetrator could never be eliminated, but in an offence this heinous in nature, it was not a natural assumption that a woman had carried out such a bloodcurdling crime. Beheadings *by* women were almost unheard of in any country. At the same time, murders of women by men ran the gamut when it came to cause: from suspicion of infidelity to issues of property all the way up to a badly made breakfast. Who were the lucky ones to escape these fates? And in this Adhiban case, the rape itself was only one of the crimes; the other was the grievous physical assault upon the woman and then, the brother – how is one to gauge which crime left a lasting impact?

She had her doubts about two characters of the cast in particular – something did not seem right about what they had said. Her right-hand man, Havildar Panneerselvam, who was an upright officer, over two decades in the profession, was convinced that the accused's friend Rajalakshmi had a role in the murder and disappearance. Asha scratched her chin and looked closely at the thick case file – while that notion could not be dismissed, something told her the friend was all wrath and fulmination and perhaps even capable of helping out the accused, her dear friend, but given the transparent and uninhibited way she had expressed her rage, it was unlikely she was a conspirator or an accomplice. Plus, Asha reasoned, there was something about Sriveni which suggested that she would not take any of her loved ones' help and then disappear, leaving them behind to be held criminally culpable. That left the two people Asha was a little more interested in than the others.

She pulled out the individual reports based on testimonies of the family members. The preamble in each report itself ran to just a page, sometimes less, typed out by a constable at the station and in not very clear or eloquent expression. Asha shook her head despondently: they never properly teach report-writing skills – it is paramount for a police officer to know how to write a report, because a bad report, or poorly filled-in, or worse, inaccurately filled-in report, could be thrown out by a court and an accused can go scot-free as a consequence of police ineptitude. The reports in front of her were written in the most decrepit prose, riddled with typos, and for every sentence that had been transcribed from the audio tapes, Asha wondered how many had been left out. The team of police officers she had sent out to speak with Sriveni's family and neighbours had, on Asha's express instructions, worked in *mufti* (the police uniform always being far more threatening and overwhelming when it came to coaxing civilians to speak up), taking a local woman along so as to break down family members' resistance to speaking with the police. Her experience had shown her that when it came to violence against women, it was best to work *with* members of the aggrieved family rather than *against* them, especially at the information-gathering stage. And in this most baffling of cases, where both the accused and the head of the victim were missing, it was essential to get the *facts* of the case right. But now, looking at the threadbare reports on her table, Asha rued the many slippages of the investigative process that bedevilled policework in India, and as she scanned the desultory prose, her mind worked double time to join the dots, to memorize, to collect, sift, parse, and draw a tentative mental map of the crime.

Police-speak had the tendency to flatten all voices and Asha often relied on her field experience and her knowledge of Tamil Nadu and its people to humanize and amplify what she was reading. An ability to combine hard-nosed detective work with a penchant for analysing social problems had shown her that a homicide investigation was not always about causes and effects; it required critical imagination, logical and lateral thinking, even a flight or two of inspired fancy, all the while coordinating, calibrating and shifting facts, premises, conclusions like a card-sharper moves his playing deck before the watchful eyes of his patrons: if you missed a trick, the game was lost. This cat-and-mouse play is what kept her firmly anchored in her job, the work of unravelling a mystery, an unknown, far outscoring the everyday brutality she had learned, on the job, to confront and work through. And at the end of the day, all she had when she went back – at whatever ungodly hour – to her bed and to her fitful sleep, was the hope that behind the thrill, the ugliness, the labour and the toil lay justice. That hope – thinnest of all hopes – was the fuel that kept her going, and with each case she cracked, Asha learned more about human desires, privations and psychologies, and it was always this sedimented knowledge – collected over years of painstaking police work – that came to her aid in solving cases. Until now, that is.

Reproaching herself for losing track, Asha went back to the reports. She might have been, in another birth, a philosopher but policework had made her a firm rationalist, a total pragmatist. When she saw a problem, she could only look for solutions; when she encountered a mystery, she had to go looking for its heart. This case presented her with both: a problem and a mystery. And she only had these materials in front of her to make sense of it all. The sensational nature of this case, the public outcry and political pressure meant that Asha had recourse to some unusual bonuses: for instance, the recce teams that visited Sittanavasal residents and Sriveni's family members were equipped with a portable recorder each, which enabled Asha to have a store of audio testimonies. After reading each report, Asha listened attentively to the set of tapes, the laborious job of playing, rewinding, forwarding the audio nearly as toilsome as the wretched report-reading and the mental work of assembling, disassembling and reassembling facts. The more she heard the tapes, the more she was dismayed at the amount of information missing in the transcribed reports, the merest of outlines of the gruesome crime, all but vanishing on the typed pages in a jumble of unpatterned details. And Asha realized, no matter how much technology you give a policeman, if he cannot write a proper report, everything is for nought!

Refusing to let her annoyance overwhelm her process, Asha resolved to speak to the constable but baulked at the thought of engaging with the SHO, T. P. Kanagaratnam, a man whose years in the police had converted him into the most cynical of officers she had met. The SHO was already miffed that under the weight of a public outcry, the case had been transferred to an ACP, but he was doubly annoyed when the ACP turned out to be a woman. Asha was no stranger to the behaviour of junior-ranking male officers whose outer self was one of deference to rank but whose body language and facial expressions often maintained a sullen insubordination, an acquiescing insolence that was always offered as a rise to her. Over the years, she had learned to not take the bait, to maintain eye contact and an unflinching professionalism in her own demeanour, and with time and dogged success, she had steadily built a reputation as a crack investigator and a no-nonsense and impersonal officer of the law. It helped that in a state like Tamil Nadu, her command over English also had high premium and she was much sought-after at state-level events in schools and colleges where she gave speeches encouraging the youth, especially young girls, to aim for IPS and join the Indian Police. But on nights like this one, all her prowess and experience were on trial.

That SHO at Pudukottai was old-school: in the aftermath of the attack on Sriveni, he and his team had roughed up Murali, one of the accused in the gangrape case, but Murali was low-hanging fruit, and his interrogation did not go much further. Eventually, all the accused in the gangrape case were acquitted by the court because of the shambolic way in which the investigation had been conducted. There was room for appeal but, as is often the fate of such cases, the arduous and convoluted process had broken the back of the family and they did not follow up after the verdict. Asha had the 1998 K. Sriveni files before her, but she resolved to check other related police records for the year too. She half-anticipated what she would find: witnesses turning hostile, poorly conducted interviews, errors in medical reports or misplaced reports, contradictory evidence strengthening the alibis of some of the accused, etc., etc. The gangrape case had made headlines for a while in the local news and in the Tamil papers and TV programmes, but it did not break through to English-language outlets, and in a year or so, civic memory diminished as public outrage shifted to other crimes and issues. This was the familiar trajectory unfortunately of many cases of crime against women. But as an officer of the law, Asha could not afford to lose her trust in the law, and despite her own growing cynicism in the profession, she also tried hard to nurture a real commitment to justice and truth, fuzzy as these ideals always were.

Kanagaratnam's own report was in front of her. It outlined an uncomplicated explanation of the case. In fact, in one of their awkward chats, he had recommended rounding up the husband and two brothers and to question them for Sriveni's whereabouts. She knew what he meant by 'question' but stayed quiet. His own sympathies were with the woman, she recognized, but his allegiance was to the political bigwigs, which led to a schizophrenic attitude in the man towards the whole case. Consequently, he offered Asha 'the best solution': round up some local or non-local ruffians, then grab a known *goonda* or two who held enmity towards Adhiban (and on this score, the SHO had an embarrassment of riches – Adhiban had led a charming life, in the course of which he had earned many enemies) and simply 'encounter' them. Kanagaratnam even offered a few of his men for the job.

This was a school of thinking in the police Asha was familiar with by now. Although initially she would be outraged by the encounter specialists in the force, over the years, she had learned to adroitly work her way around such men and their anarchic methods. But Kanagaratnam was not your average bloodthirsty cop who thought the badge and uniform gave him the power to dole out justice, she had to give him that. Not for him the populist but dangerous vigilante machismo of Rajni and Vijay films. He was more wily, more ripened in the ways of the world, and in his own fashion – with four daughters and several granddaughters, whom he adored – he was sensitive to issues surrounding the protection of women, and so long as he did not have to salute a female officer, in his own orthodox manner, he was a champion of women's rights as outlined in the lawbooks. This was the man who recommended not going by the book in this case and to simply arrest someone in place of the missing Sriveni, slap the charges on him and be done with it all in a trumped-up encounter. With clinical precision, he outlined the way it could be done as well – a deserted stretch of the road on the way to the district magistrate, an attempted escape by the arrested man or men when the police vehicle blew a tire, which would lead to police firing out of self-defence. It had taken all of her self-restraint to meet Kanagaratnam's eye and tell him to arrange, instead, a small task force of officers whom she would like to brief before they went into Sittanavasal for further questioning. By pretending to not hear his expert recommendation, Asha was doing the man, and herself, a kindness – if she reported him, he would have one helluva bureaucratic problem two years away from retirement *and* this was not a thing she wanted to be known among her officers for. By refusing the 'encounter' method, she might be standing with the right and the lawful but by tarnishing the career of another officer, she would only earn the contempt of her colleagues. There was no point to such pulls of sympathy; she had to find a way to get to Sriveni and bring her to the station to face the law.

Asha adjusted the headphones and began to hear the testimonies once more. The husband.

The husband was a curious figure because he did not display the usual or expected resentment or despair of one whose honour has been besmirched, whose wife has been raped and has gone mad thereafter or whatever it is her illness could be called. He showed no excess of emotion – either by way of anger or tears – what *was* it about his reaction that was gnawing away at her? Of course, there is no one answer as to what is the *right* reaction to something as catastrophic as what happened to the woman and her family, but his whole turn to philosophy and guru-speak just didn't cut it for her. On the one hand, it was possible that the man could not face up to the enormity of his family's devastation; on the other, it was also possible that at his core, he, like most Indian men brought up in the lap of patriarchal values, was not capable of reasoning that goes against the system which guaranteed his privileges, and chose to turn apathetic because, well, maybe a kind of numbness set in? Or perhaps that was not it at all, and to take a less venal view of the man, was it possible, that like most human beings at the lower ends of the social ladder, he had simply been rendered mute by both the unpunished brutality against his wife (and co-brother) as well as the continued failure of the judicial system to bring the criminals to justice? Was it not conceivable that he didn't have the revenge gene, which his wife apparently did? That might also explain their inability to keep the marriage going after the wife's physical recovery. Perhaps there was no attendant mental or marital recovery and they shattered and scattered as two different people. It was not unheard of that a marriage disintegrated in the face of a major tragedy that detonated their life open.

Asha sighed and looked at her watch. Her ex-husband had given it to her on their sixth anniversary – the last they had spent together. It was now four years to the fact; he had remarried, had a son and was living happily in his new posting in northern India. She, on the other hand, was married to her job and had remained faithful to it. Asha got up to make herself some coffee – it was a bad idea this late into the night, but something told her, this case would not allow sleep anyway, not until her thoughts had been arranged and her impressions recorded properly. From her kitchen window, she saw the bright moon, large and ponderous, shining full into the clear night. There was a light wind rustling through the dark trees and the night cries of bats and cicadas hung incipiently in the air.

She made her coffee light, black, without sugar, and went back to the dining table where the pages of a woman's life were spread out like so many dead butterflies.

Asha sipped her cup thoughtfully. The papers looked like the aftermath of a small bomb – like this case, there was so much debris it was hard to pick out the bits that mattered. Unmindfully, she rearranged the tapes back in their box, a repurposed carton made of cardboard, and was struck by the thought, suddenly, that all this, right here, was a person's whole life, as remembered, distilled and retold by those that knew her. A stack of papers and some fifteen spools of tape: Asha had the feeling that she was rummaging through ashes looking for a clue, something to know and understand the person that Sriveni was. She wondered if the woman was alive or dead, and unexpectedly, she felt rueful at the thought of never catching her, of never meeting her, of never finding out. She wondered too what capturing Sriveni would accomplish – maybe the woman had relocated and found herself a new home, a new beginning: wasn't that everyone's secret desire – to just up and leave one's whole life and begin afresh?

As she felt her head clear, Asha began organizing the files in rows, moving them about like pieces on a chess board. She thought of the husband's disappearances: where was he going to and coming back from? Why not return to the home where he and his wife had stayed in or to his in-laws' place where his daily meals would be assured? Better still, why not return to his parents' hometown and stay there? What was causing his unexplained itinerancy? This aspect would have to be looked into. Did he have a hand in his wife's disappearance and were his periodic visits and returns tied to keeping her out of sight? What had he said: 'but it's a story for everyone and to each his own version' – what did multiple versions of any story mean? About anything in the world, there is one truth, Asha's work had shown her, but there were several ways of *telling* that truth. Was the husband implying more here than met the eye?

And all that philosophical talk about life and karma and whatnot seemed dubious in a schoolteacher, especially one who taught mathematics. Something altogether fuzzy and abstract in a man who must be used to precision and accuracy and clarity. Of course, mathematician-philosophers have existed, both in western and eastern traditions, but was *this* man one? Asha had her doubts.

She also recalled the father from the report – a traumatized man, wounded perhaps beyond repair by the loss of his daughter's innocence, by the gruesomeness of the attacks on both daughter and son, a man, by his own account, average and without ambition. He too showed a penchant for the philosophical. What was it about men, some men, she corrected herself, that they turn to philosophizing after something visceral jolts their world-view, their structure of existence? Did Sriveni have recourse, as these men did, to some larger-than-life understanding of the world, of her self, her life, and that of others? Do women, some women at least, transcend the nets of material life for something over-and-beyond? Asha rapped the file with her pencil hard: how was any kind of transcendence possible? What options do ordinary women have? Her work brought her in frequent interaction with women related in some form or the other with crime – most often as victims, next as witnesses, but also frequently enough as conspirators and accomplices and finally, less commonly but notably nonetheless, as perpetrators. But in all cases, one thread ran with more or less conspicuous regularity and that was women's sense of entrapment, of being held back, monitored, surveilled, or otherwise denied and marginalized: this was a viscerally felt, shared feeling in women from a cross-section of social backgrounds. But even as she was coming to this sobering idea, Asha's eye fell on a passport-size photograph of Sriveni's younger brother and his current condition as a mentally challenged mute reminded her that a male-centred society could very well turn upon its favoured kind, and men, some men, too can suffer dire consequences for going against the established order.

The coffee was helping her gain focus. There were many threads to this story and suddenly, Asha felt that *prima facie* was tugging her in one direction, but there were forces lying beneath the surface and there, another drama was unfolding. Thinking of the elder brother, Asha pulled out his report; elder, she reflected, was a strange way to call someone only seven minutes older than his twin. Be that as it may, the elder brother also didn't add up. On the one hand, there was all that sentiment about his twin brother and then his remarkable detachment from his sister, so much so that he ended up cursing her. Was that a credible move? Why was the younger brother so clearly outraged and despairing while the older one's reaction was so circumspect, maybe even unsympathetic? Or was it? Was he responding in contrary fashion to his brother's excessive emotion and the perilous fallout of that? Perhaps he did not have a natural affinity for his sister and was now torturing himself over it. After all, simply because one is related by blood doesn't mean that you and your sibling love each other. Still, what to make of his confessing to his inability to prevent the attack on his sister or feel invested in her recovery or do anything practical for the family –

all of this, was it a fool's gambit? Or was it a reflection of his true state of being? He seemed a lot angrier and more devastated over his brother's condition. Why didn't he react in the same way over the brutal attack on his sister? Is the distance between a brother and a sister so vast in comparison to that between a brother and another that one can choose to be moved by the privations of only one and not the other? Was it a reflection of a distance forged by gender in a patriarchal world or was this a matter of chance – that this guy just happened to be distant from his sister?

Asha's mind drew up an image of her own brother, younger to her by six years, but in all respects, a tremendous caregiver and support to her. It was he who had always championed her decisions – what was it about their lives that made him the way he was and Sriveni's *thambi* so different? She wondered if it was a question of class and education: her brother had studied in elite schools and colleges where he mingled with boys and girls, had been exposed to multiple cultures, and had imbibed what she thought was a liberal outlook. And yet, she recalled a major fight in his home when he had put his foot down against his wife's idea of getting a tattoo somewhere on her body. It seemed to be a simple enough affair, a small thing easily resolved one way or another, but her brother's recalcitrance and adamancy had taken her by surprise, and his wife, after yet another row one evening, had turned up at Asha's doorstep with a small suitcase to stay for a few days. It had taken all of Asha's diplomatic skills to effect a reconciliation between the two over what seemed like a childish fit in a world full of adult woes. Where was class and education in all of this assertion of control over a woman's body and her will, Asha wondered. The question of gender was not simple at all, and the picture was never as clear as oppressor and victim on two sides divided by a clear boundary.

Listening to the tapes gave Asha a thick sense of who Sriveni was to different members of her family, what each one thought of her, how they reconciled her disappearance with what they knew of her – but was she more than the sum total of these parts? Is not everyone that way? What is a woman when she is not a daughter, sister, wife, mother? What was she beyond a teacher, companion, colleague? Asha felt that the more she learned about Sriveni, the more that woman escaped her grasp. The elder brother and the husband were both intriguing, but most intriguing of all was Sriveni herself, the missing centre of this whole case. *Who* was she? *What* was she like? She seemed to be many things to many people, and several aspects to her seemed credible and knowable. In

Sriveni, Asha saw a reflection of a standard type of Indian woman, perhaps even herself, but was it a true reflection? After all, the standard type of Indian woman does not go around decapitating men. But then, wryly, Asha thought, perhaps she would, if the fear of getting caught were to be removed. And at that exact point, an idea struck her: what if Sriveni's act was timed precisely so because she had found a way to overcome the fear of capture? Had she found a route of escape because of which she then decided to go ahead with the murder of Adhiban? Why wait for four years to do what she did, although admittedly she was neither in the physical nor mental condition to avenge her brutal attack? 1998 to 2002. But why now? Surely, the assault on the brother only two months ago *had* to be the catalytic event, precipitating her murderous act – wasn't it? Or, contrary to all such premeditation, did Sriveni find her own thorny path to some semblance of self, a path that detached her from all sense and foreboding of consequences so that she did it anyway, out of furious revenge, undiminished by time and undeterred by the fear of capture and jail? And why only stop at one man and let the others go? What next – had she vanished or was she planning a second attack upon the remaining men? Both Raji and the husband had alluded to the fear and horror of the remaining men, as if they sensed that Sriveni's vendetta was not over. Could they be knowing more than they were letting on? And *where* was Sriveni? Police had been going through Sittanavasal town with a fine-toothed comb. It was clear she could not be hiding in the town – had she escaped to another city, but how and with whose help? Where could an ordinary schoolteacher go? In the coming days, would her body be found somewhere – could she have committed suicide in some remote place now that her vengeance seemed to have been satisfied and she was certain to be jailed and probably sentenced to life imprisonment? Even for a sympathetic judge who did not favour the death sentence, a beheading would be hard to ignore, and he or she could not be seen publicly as tolerating or condoning it. A beheading was, in the hands of a woman, an act of terror as catastrophic as blowing up a tower – if one did it in the name of retributive justice, would not a second, then a third, and many others follow? And then where would this system be? But perhaps, it was not Sriveni at all who did this, but some sympathizer, a family member, and she had finally found her peace. Could that be it? Had Sriveni, in fact, escaped to a new life, a new identity, and was this going to be one of those crimes that the police set aside, after some years of indifferent investigation, as a cold case even though there is no statute of limitations on murder, especially of a monstrous kind? Which of these two types exactly *was* Sriveni?

Asha was asking the right questions, she felt, but *answers* still eluded her. That said, asking the right questions was important – perhaps the most important thing of all.

The mother and the grandmother seemed to think of Sriveni as exceptional, and Asha looked at their reports again. Sriveni's medical experience made her very interesting as did her background as a geography teacher in the local school. She was an educated woman with a sound traditional knowledge of medical recovery and much experience in medicinal practice related to women's bodies. Perhaps it is a mistake to think of Sriveni as ordinary, as a typical or standard victim, Asha conjectured. She went back to the tapes and heard the grandmother's testimony once more: the bit about the way in which Sriveni, in the midst of her gangrape, had prevented her injuries from becoming fatal stood out to her. How did the grandmother know this? Medical records from the hospital had enumerated every single injury upon Sriveni's body and there were multiple reports of tests and physicians' conclusions, but not one doctor had documented anything significant about the injuries as a whole or spotted any larger pattern with regard to the nature of the injuries themselves. The grandmother had seen the injuries from a different angle, telling a tale of endurance and desperate resourcefulness. It was not unknown for women after such a ferocious attack to be found in a vegetative state, from which they never recovered – the appalling Aruna Shanbaug case came to Asha's mind, a case all police officers study closely during their training at the academy in Hyderabad. Sriveni had somehow managed to stave off such a fate by anticipating correctly and countering the men's frenzied assault in the limited ways she could. If she was such a remarkable woman, would it be too far-fetched to think that the murder of Adhiban was one she had been planning and preparing for all through the past years? If that were the case, what caused her to do it now, at the precise time that she did do it? *What was her thinking here*, Asha turned the facts over and over in her mind. Is it possible for a woman to show such extraordinary, superhuman ability, as the grandmother says Sriveni did, especially in the midst of such violence and violation? And what of her painful, long and difficult recovery thereafter? Does one truly recover? How many years does a woman take to get over a sexual violation that was also a ghastly assault causing untold bodily and mental trauma? Or does one become permanently unhinged? But in that case, if one becomes unhinged – as, it seemed to Asha, every single family member of Sriveni's had – is it possible for one such to meticulously plan and carry out a scheme of revenge?

With a jolt, Asha realized that she had completely forgotten a crucial detail: the miscarriage! She rummaged through the pages to find the hospital report: when Sriveni was wheeled into the city hospital, she had already lost a lot of blood and the resident doctor's report recorded: *large blood clots containing foetus, likely just under four months, length 11.7 cm, weight 12 grams; red, pink, brown blood and amniotic fluid all over clothes.* Asha scanned a few other pages and found the report of the doctor who conducted the post-mortem on the foetus – the report confirmed that it was healthy and well on its way to life, until the attack killed it. How did the miscarriage factor into this crime? Was it catalytic in its own way – but four years after the rape and assault? A period of painful recovery for Sriveni that, Asha surmised, must have been its own journey to hell and back. She wondered if the men involved knew that Sriveni was pregnant at the time – at four months, often a woman does not show and it is hard to know from the outside. Something about this train of thought arrested her reverie. She pinched the bridge of her nose hard, the force causing her eyes to shut tight and after a few moments, as she removed her fingers, waves of release counteracted the pressure inside her head.

The final forensic reports were still awaited, and they would confirm whose hair was found in the burnt residue, but Asha could not put her finger on the whole business of burning the hair. One aspect was clear: everyone believed Sriveni had unusually beautiful hair and the first witnesses who claimed to have seen her walking with, what looked to them like a man's head, singled out her swaying tresses, making for a striking image that they spoke of almost reverentially, as if describing a much-feared goddess. Her hair was a marker of her uniqueness; by shearing it off and burning it before disappearing with Adhiban's head, what message was Sriveni sending and to whom? For sure, the burnt hair and clothes ensured that beyond that point, the sniffer dogs were no good. And then, there was something deeply unsettling about the younger brother Chinna too. Asha searched out the elder brother's report, where he said that, of late, Chinna had taken to dressing in the sister's sarees and walking about town like a madman. Was there some twisted tale here, Asha wondered, of the brothers, or maybe perhaps even just Chinna, aiding and abetting the sister, all the while pretending to be mad? Was he truly mentally incapable of committing a crime or was it all a facade, a preparation for something else? And if Sriveni had truly disappeared, was there a sequel to come for the remaining men? Should the police force prepare for the return of an avenging angel or should they be looking for a dead body? Asha felt cloven between two extremes in this truly confounding case and all her instincts told her that truth lay somewhere in between, under the surface of things – but *where?* She couldn't shake off the feeling that common to all the testimonies she had read was the belief among the family members that Sriveni had somehow escaped – or was she over-reading? Perhaps their sense of confusion was as real as their belief in Sriveni's abilities – but were the two views of Sriveni compatible? Asha's training and insight had reached a dead end, for as long as Sriveni remained missing, there really was no accounting for the crime, no way to prepare for the future, no closure for the families left behind. A question she had heard in one of the testimonies – wasn't it Raji's – hovered diaphanously at the edges of her mind: *How many of us must go missing before you notice?*

The grandmother! Asha rummaged and pulled out the grandmother's report once more – in an offhand comment on the margins, the constable who transcribed the tape had written in pen that the grandmother had made an observation about whether the men had known or not that Sriveni was carrying. (Was the policeman wondering if this exonerated the men from the additional brutality of the unborn's death? Asha could not be sure.) She put the headphones on, and as Asha heard again the grandmother's words, she too wondered whether it would have made a difference that night. Did the men know? Would it have mattered? Who could say for certain? Her heart was solemn and cold, as Asha pictured Sriveni as the victim of multiple miscarriages: not only the miscarriage that led to the loss of her child, but the miscarriage of a basic minimum human decency at the hands of the attackers, and perhaps worst of all, the miscarriage of justice by the judicial system. In the 1998 files, there was no police record of the unborn child whose death in the brutal attack did not feature in the prosecution's case at all because at under sixteen weeks, it did not, as per Indian law, qualify for personhood. There were so many wrongs here, Asha slowly and sorrowfully realized, and at the centre of it all was Sriveni – the absent presence, known to her now only by the traces the woman had left behind.

It was past 3 a.m. and the night sky was inching towards day. The stars had receded and the moon looked pallid, helpless before the rising sun. An extreme crime is always a flashpoint, Asha thought: in the sudden, blinding light of its blaze, one saw many things in clarity, but the light is so tremendous that it generates multiple shadows itself and it is possible for one to be caught in the grip of these dark spaces, where nothing is clear, all statements are confounding, and all conclusions potential falsehoods, total misprisions. And in the aftershock of the blinding flash, the eye suffers for long the consequences, the illusions of dark where there is none, the half-moons and fragments of light and clear that float away the closer you move towards them, all of it rendering normal sight difficult for several moments after the fact. And if this were a metaphor for life itself, how terrifically prone must she be to constant misinterpretation and misreading, how likely it is that she may have got it all wrong, after all. It was a bitter notion to close the files on; Asha knew it would be a long road to a short sleep. But tomorrow was another day – surely, there would be news of the woman, or a development. In crime, there always is something – one only has to persevere, she knew. Then again, how long could one keep on looking until they were assigned to the next case? The clamour for a quick resolution was unrelenting, but Asha was set upon finding a missed clue or a new lead – the next few days were going to be critical: she had to keep looking. The last thing she saw as she closed a thick file was a newspaper clipping of the beheading that the constable had for some reason pinned to the final chargesheet of the gangrape case.

The New I

Friday, August 30, 2002

Man beheaded, head missin

Pudukottai: In a horrific incident, a man was beheaded outside a local bar in Pudukottai district of Tamil Nadu on Thursday. According to early witness reports, the gruesome act was carried out allegedly by a woman who walked three kilometres with the chopped head to the local temple. According to the police, the deceased, identified as S. Adhiban, a resident of Sittanavasal town, was the local school patron and a party worker in the regional All India Tamilakam (AIT).

The accused woman, K. Sriveni, worked as a teacher at the local school and was allegedly seen walking with the severed head. She has since disappeared and police have launched a district-wide search for the missing woman and the head of the deceased.

According to the police, in 1998, Sriveni had accused Adhiban

Re
fol
im

Th
th
rel
th
be
of
ex
in
its
be
co
or

It
tot
thi
de

11

ONE OF HER BELOVED SPOTS AFTER THE LUSH Garden was a part of the cave that took Veni completely by surprise, but by now she had learned that the rules that measured her life above were often in abeyance inside the cave. Here, nature had free rein and she was the humble recipient of its munificence. On one of her long walks, now with a thick stick which aided her in the rocky, stony parts in prising out yielding paths, Veni came upon a tremendous waterfall. Not only was gushing water coming out of a cliff face as tall as the skies, but the water ran as a river which spread far and wide, disappearing into different regions of the cave. Veni now understood that the pool that greeted her when she first came into the cave must be fed by a train of subterranean aquifers made by this waterfall.

A rock spot from across the falls became her chosen haunt. It was large enough for her to lie down in and with the roar of the water in her ears, Veni often caught some of her soundest sleep there. For months, it had been hard for her to sleep, so hard, in fact, that she had taken to some fifty naps a day. Darkness only brought the horrors of tortuous, labyrinthine nightmares and for many nights during her recovery, she could sleep only for a few minutes or so. Her night-time terrors pained her husband, she knew, but how could she help it? He had always been so outside her and there was now no opening certain doors. But here, next to the fall, it was miraculous how quickly sleep came to her, especially with the sound of water hitting rock, the wind brushing through the trees, and with the slow, soporific sunlight on one's face, it was so much easier to sleep here. In this world away from her home, inside the cave's many pools, or floating in the river formed by the waterfall, Veni would drift like a baby inside its mother's amniotic home, buoying along, bumping gently into the rounded rocks, arms spread out like she was flying in water with the barest of motion. There was a sweet release in such moments and she could simply let go.

On all days, the waterfall was a magnificent sight, but on some days, special beyond words, the fall became awe-inspiring: when the wind blew inside the cave at a terrific pace, it tended to spoon the water aloft in a kind of reverse spray and for several minutes, the entire waterfall, in an act that defied gravity, fell upwards. When Veni first witnessed the reverse waterfall, she clapped in joy, unable to stop herself from jumping like a small child watching her favourite toy go. She laughed aloud as her heart soared at the sight of the water spraying upwards, some of which the wind scattered all around, sousing her own face and arms in a fine film of wetness. At other times, the tumbling water shattered into the rocks below like pellets of glass or mercury, so shiny, so many. From her vantage on the rock, Veni saw that the cliff face behind the waterfall was cut in deep, creating a kind of room that, with some rope and nimble, careful walking, she could possibly reach. In such a case, she would witness the waterfall from *within*! She prepared mentally for such an adventure. She would need specific things, supplies that would enable the precarious walk and she wrote down a brief list of items to bring along the next time.

She was always curious to look for new entrances and exits to the cave. Steadily, over time, she found well-concealed mouths that were overgrown with weeds or covered by natural walls of rock. The entrance that she had serendipitously found was similar, and it was a wonder that she had found it at all. At a steep angle on the rock face that could send a casual ambler plunging into the stones over eighty feet below, the entrance Veni found was naturally well-hidden. And had it not been for her decision that day, so precipitate she now knew, to risk a look, just a glimpse maybe, at the face of death, had it not been for a momentary surrender to despair, Veni may never have ventured as far out, away from the *kovil*, as she did. Nonetheless, but for that one decision, at the brink of suicide, she had been saved by the most miraculous thing: the opening to the cave. On that day, she had stepped out looking for some quiet, for, of late, there was a sound in her head that refused to go away – like the grinding of one's teeth, a tight, compressed sound as if gravel were being crunched inside her mouth but not of her own will, and slowly, that sound built up and grew tighter, more intense, inside her face, near the centre of her forehead so that when she screwed shut her eyes in defence, scrunching up her face, the sound travelled to her brain and boomed inside her skull's bony walls. In fact, that sound was always there, in the background on the best of days, but on others, on the ghastly days beyond enduring, days of cold in hot weather and hot in cold rain, on those days, it was right there in the foreground, driving her to distraction. It was one such dreadful day that she had stormed out of her home looking for some peace and quiet, walking all the way up the high rocks towards the temple, past the abode of gods and the spectral monks, towards the very edge. And at the edge, she had found the cave's mouth and it had changed her life utterly.

All it would take is a landslip for the cave to reclaim its open mouth and shut itself forever. As she wandered inside, Veni speculated about the temple above, itself an accretion upon a Jaina monastery dating from many centuries ago and cut into the rock face. Sittanavasal or the Abode of Great Saints, as it was called, had also become a temple, *kovil*, and the townspeople approached the Jaina burial ground and rock frescoes with the same devotion as they did the Hindu gods. Occasionally, the government woke up to the place's heritage and sent teams of people for restoration work like cleaning, glazing, plastering and so on. When that happened, the town would be abuzz with activity for several days, new people always bringing new business, new needs. A team leader, usually an elderly archaeologist, would hold camps to impress upon people the need to catch vandals, protect the rock temple and ensure no one entered certain parts. The townsfolk would hear such speeches patiently: no one really went exploring the caves to look at old, peeling walls. Even the frescoes were in tatters so there wasn't much to look at. It was always somewhat puzzling to them why city cats, university scholars and government officials put so much store by what time was ravaging anyway. Thus, until Veni took upon herself to explore the cave complex, especially from below, no soul had stirred to look beyond the evident. Perhaps she should have listened to the experts more closely, but having come to know the cave-world on her own, Veni felt remote from the kind of knowledge that the team of scholars and officers of the state brought to the town. How did it matter if the frescoes dated from the first century or the seventh? Who cared whether it was a Pallava king or a tribe of mendicants that had repurposed the rock into a habitable complex? These were not the right questions, Veni thought. One ought to ask, for instance, what made the water in the cave so sweet and nourishing? Why did her town, several towns, in fact, have to suffer through a water crisis every year? What role could humans play in their natural environment that did not degrade it until the whiplash of their excesses recoiled upon the community itself? We are following the wrong trail; we are lost in a wilderness of our making, she fretted.

The cave had become a home for her, and her family grew accustomed to her long absences. Aatha was bedridden and increasingly growing taciturn; Amma was distracted by the smallest things; Appa walked with his head bowed; and her husband, fellow teacher, the sharer of her life until that day everything changed – well, he was nowhere to be seen. She heard from the fish-seller that he had been spotted in town, checking out of a hotel. But she had not seen him nor had he sought her out. It made things easier for Veni. Alone, what could she not do? In that frame of mind, she began to home herself in the cave. She had grown to enjoy the many kinds of fruits, berries and leaves found in the cave, learning which to eat and how much, avoiding the ones that could be poisonous or lethal. The reddish-orange beads of jujube, *elanthai pazham* and the decadent *mankustan* were her favourites, the latter especially of such exquisite flavour that one pined in memory of it. When ripe, the mankustan, called the queen of fruits, was a dusky purple like the monsoon sky just before an inky downpour, but once you prised open its deceitfully hard outer shell, you met the softest, most delicate white fruit in the shape of a flower, with its soft plump skin about to burst with nectarine sweetness. Elsewhere in the cave, there grew wood apple trees whose fruit Amma used to make jams and preserves. And in an area of the doline which gave way to a new chain of caves, the soil was a coarse, gravelly red, and there grew abundantly the *kodukkapuli*, whose bark, seeds and pulp Aatha used liberally in her medicinal concoctions. Its peculiar fruit ripened to a dark red and looked halfway between a fat peapod and a sumptuous *jilebi*, the coily and twisty pods enclosing numerous seeds covered in a white edible pulp that caused your tongue to hit the palate in a tang. Once aplenty, many of these fruits had now become rare in her town's main market and it was with a new sense of joy that inside the cave, Veni rediscovered her childhood tastes.

A profusion of massive plantains covered large areas of the cave and they were not only useful for their enormous leaves which provided shelter for bats and flycatchers and swifts, but they also yielded bananas of various types and sizes, a nimiety of offerings that the insects, birds, and small animals thrived on. Veni also found a special kind of edible mushroom nestled halfway inside the bark of a log and half-growing into the soft, yielding soil. Its head was smooth and a glossy light brown. She pulled out the small caramel-topped mushroom, surprisingly tightly embedded so she had to put some force into it. It plopped out and she scraped off the soil that had come along, and with her knife, she bruised its stem lightly to reveal a light blue tinge. Washing it gingerly, she plucked some pieces of the mushroom and tucked them inside a red banana from one of the plantains, the impromptu dish having become, in time, a favourite of hers, after eating which for hours she felt nourished and tranquil. Veni knew the caramel-topped mushroom had special powers; in her town, there was an underground trade in it and the locals used the mushroom to achieve a temporary high. It grew only in specific places and was very rare, so the chances of finding one in a random mushroom hunt was low, and there were boys who knew exactly where and how to find these special, 'magic' ones.

Everything in the cave seemed charmed, not just the mushrooms. There was something in the vegetation all round that helped to relax her mind and her spirit, yet energizing her later for long walks of discovery. Many were the hours she spent in regrounding herself surrounded by trees, water and light, and from such moments, she would rise feeling euphoric, as if she could accomplish anything in life. It seemed to her in such moments that a crushing weight was lifting from the centre of her being and she was finally breathing. Her doctors had given her a regimen for recovery: she was to isolate her symptoms, chart their onset and duration, inform family members and enlist support, and treat them as they came in a manner outlined by the therapy manuals, an approach that was fine if one's mind were an object of scrutiny to be studied in a closed laboratory under the lens of whatever science was being employed. But signs of her illness never arrived with forewarning or discretely, coming often instead in a rush with a welter of other terrors, as an assault that left her feeling like a tangled madness of inchoate thoughts and cavernous yearnings not unlike the wild formations of the roots of a tree or the entwined snarly grass with its profusion of mud and insects and mushrooms and fungi that made up the ground in many parts of the doline. If one were like such a ground, how was it possible to detach a single component from the others to study it or understand it in isolation? Is it possible, Veni wondered in the clarifying haze brought on by her magical mushroom, that the columns and doors and windows she saw in her mind's eye, the expanding and contracting circles and fractal-like passageways, were all permutations and combinations of a single consciousness? But whose? Was it nature's or hers?

This was no passive guidance either, Veni began to comprehend as she walked the length and breadth of the cave and its world within. Anyone who has taken a stroll through a jungle or a garden can sense the intelligence of the space – there is a continuous conversation going on between the plants and the millions of organisms – simple and complex – that draw their life from the plants and, in return, provide to plants a range of services. This dialogue, Veni intuited, lay at the very heart of natural life. Once Appa had shown her the fruiting of mushrooms in sporing season, an evanescent spray emanating from the mushroom head, to see which one had to catch the light at a particular angle or you could miss it entirely. Veni remembered lying on the dewy grass, trying to listen to Appa attentively as he scraped the wood gently to show her how mushrooms proliferated. She recalled the black powder that puffed into the air when Appa squeezed the pod-shaped mushrooms, thousands and thousands of spores carried by the eddies of the wind to new places, looking for moisture, where, upon falling, they would root and, in time, sprout into baby mushrooms. As children, she, Raji and her brothers would run around catching 'Grandfather's beard', the *appooppanthadi* spores of the milkweed tree, pods with fine filaments that flew far and wide in the air carrying seeds for germination. Appa called this the language of revival and persistence in nature and told her that it was as important as one's own breathing.

In her sojourns to the parallel world, Veni began to see the many truths embedded in her father's early lessons. Sporing and fruiting formed a language, as did every aspect of the natural cycle, a language as unique as any of the tongues human beings had invented but far more marvellous, for these are born in nature, from nature, by and for nature. If one had to think of nature as a single consciousness, then all these different aspects were its many tongues, whose sounds and smells and sights proliferated all about us, touching every aspect of natural existence – what a miracle of life this planet was, Veni wondered in awe. When we have the power to imagine what knowledge the many tongues of natural life hold in secret, we open ourselves to being re-enchanted: not all relationships in nature are mappable and at the most enigmatic levels lie also our most nourishing realizations. The cave-world showed Veni intimations of a primordial unity, one that was manifest in the superabundance around her, but it was not a unity that had a specific form or face – like a god on a calendar. In its formlessness, it was many, variegated and ever-transforming.

The thrum and buzz of life showed her that the fragments in her consciousness, sharp as jagged glass, pieces that she saw woefully as detritus of a single, atomic self were merely the glittering surface of a privation, of her sense of irreparable loss. If she dug deeper into her mind, the walls fell away, the doors opened to new vistas, and verdant nature – with the fragrance of the flowers of her childhood – bloomed inside her mind: she had to only find a way to connect and tap into that force. On days when her distress could be quelled by such thoughts, Veni felt ready, prepared for the business of living. But on days when nothing felt reparable, she burrowed into the dark of her mind, to find a path past the lies and the delusions, to emerge on the other side, but it felt like she had entered a cave with no end, no light on the other side, only the unceasing toil of digging and tunnelling forever. On such days, the wound was mortal, nothing helped, not the walking or the mushrooms or sitting in silent communion and she learned painfully to accept such days too. Veni recalled scraps of a poem Amma sang in the months after her attack, her mother's plaintive voice reaching out like a frail faraway light in the enveloping darkness of her pain, pulling Veni out of the quagmire of the mind:

> *Yesterday,*
> *some people of this town*
> *said about me,*
> *she is the woman ...*
> *Mother heard it*
> *and asked me,*
> *'is it true?'*
> *I said, under my breath,*
> *'I'm burning.'*

Of late, she had even taken to coming into the cave in the night. Armed with a lamp, some candles and extra matches, and a small ration of food, she invariably filled her bottle with the pool's water and picked some red berries on her way. Moonlight shimmered everywhere, reflected naturally by the many pools inside. Veni walked a great deal inside. Hours flew by as she made more and more discoveries inside the doline, its fascinating world a cornucopia of natural beauties. In a small notebook that she carried in her bag, she wrote down brief descriptions and coordinates, mapping the cave-world with all the training she had as a schoolteacher, which wasn't much but was enough along with her innate pluck and intelligence. But she also knew the spots to avoid because there, the darkness was like a chokehold. The screeches from within those sections of the cave indicated the presence of large bats and she was fine with letting them be. There were so many other things in the cave to see. In the night, sometimes, these dark sections were lit up by glowworms, bats' favourite food, an ethereal sight of blue light that made it seem as if the stars had descended upon earth. But she knew better than to just blunder in and was happy to witness the beauty and mystery from afar.

The cloudburst during one of her past visits had been followed by many days of rain causing big and small pools to form in different parts of the cave. A profusion of mayflies came up one afternoon, suddenly, as the whole surface of a large pool seemed to rise as one sheet of water, a high wave, with millions and millions of mayflies flying above to find their mates and procreate. It was a wondrous sight to behold and Veni felt overwhelmed to have witnessed something so astonishingly fecund and ephemeral. Appa, who loved butterflies and moths of all kinds, had taught her about the mayflies – insects that lived for a day and whose entire existence was bound only to procreation. They did not even have stomachs and, one day, pricked by nature's mysterious rhythms – no one could predict when, where, how – they could rise, an army of several millions, in a dance that could only be choreographed by forces that were beyond the human. What made them seek out a mate? How did they know? Were they sentient, or merely following the dictates of instinct and ancient fiat? Head abuzz with questions, she stood by the water and watched the murmuration of the mayflies, like the dance of the birds she had witnessed earlier, an equally astounding and moving spectacle. Beneath the iridescent water, the fish too were caught in a frenzy for the millions of mayflies presented a sumptuous banquet.

To her father, she would have sung a ditty full of made-up lines and make-believe descriptions, he who had shown to her the magic behind the mundane, the joyous behind the banal, he who had shown her the scale of one's life.

See, father, the day darkens
behind a shimmering pall;
What gold is flung about
as if the sun were scattering
in drops of watery light,
sousing your little one so.
But my wings can fly,
Oh, your little mayfly –
Sky high, sky high, sky high!

Veni watched the mayflies heave high and low, their golden wings glimmering like scattered drops of light. *Ephemeroptera, naiad, imago* – Appa had taught her the stages of a mayfly's growth and the Greek words rolled about in her mind like so many scattered pearls, now catching the fleeting light of memory, now fading into the oblivion of a life led long ago on the shores of a vanished childhood. That these flies would not make it beyond the day made her infinitely sad, as most aspects of death did. But the Grove of the Dead had shown her that death was not the end and by dying, the mayflies lived forever. Everything became something else; transformation was the only truth about life.

The heavy rain inside the doline had wrought a miracle: one day when she walked in, she found that *neelakuṟiñci* had erupted through the cracks of the arid Grove of Death such that the whole place was covered in a blanket of pinks and blues of varying hues. How was it possible unless the plants had been lying dormant under the hard soil, all this while, waiting for rain? So that when it did come in the form of an overwhelming, all-encompassing cloudburst, over and over, it was as if the desert had bloomed. It was a silent celebration all around her, the once arid grove blooming with low, thick plants topped with thousands of the rare, precious neelakuṟiñci flowers, all huddling close like the little girls in her school, who rushed to assembly every morning, for the first five minutes or so always a torrent of sounds, as gregarious little heads joined together in glee, bumping into each other, giggling, so disarmingly innocent, unversed in the ways of the adult world and its many trials, and then growing slowly reticent, then silent, as the headmaster walked up to the makeshift stage. Veni looked at the natural wonder, overcome by a quiet reverence, and intensely conscious that she was the only one to witness it, to draw pleasure from it. But even as the thought formed in her mind, she looked up to see the thrushes and swallows flying about, and remembered all the beings of the cave, each special, incredible, capable of being itself, necessary and an indivisible part of this world. It was a colossal mistake to think that the human mind or body was at the centre of this universe – it might just be mankind's greatest delusion of grandeur. But what was she shorn of that delusion? Such a view of herself within the world humbled Veni – for suddenly, she could both be her own person and look beyond the limits of her body to her spirit that was as much of the world as it was of itself. What does it mean then to be oneself, she wondered. Am I unique? Am I irreplaceable? Am I not a mayfly of this world?

She never stayed long in one place and, with her inveterate walking, discovered newer spots to rest in and tend to. The cave-world had existed before her and would outlast her and she felt she could do nothing for it. Instead, she could utilize it, she thought, for some benefit to herself, in the manner of the great conquerors, she could try to find things to *do.* In a thicket, Veni found a resting place, and on days when her heart felt heavy from memories of loss and pain, in a little space between the roots, she would deposit flowers she had picked from all over the cave. In time, the small bed of flowers became a shrine, on which she kept a single round stone, the size of her hand and eroded by centuries of water to a smooth circular beauty, the streaky traces of its stony history etched like blood vessels under one's skin. Veni thought of her stillborn child, plucked before its time, and was glad to have given it a home. It had died above but found new life below.

On such days of quiet repair, Veni reminisced of her innermost moments of joy, a secret power that lay ensconced in her mind like a bee sleeping inside a flower, whose beauty and fragrance had the might to reach across time and fill her with a groundswell of happiness. Such moments anchored her to a sense of self, a sense of history, her history, its deep ties and friendships, to her husband and his warm embrace, to Raji, her soul sister and fellow adventurer, to her brothers so mystifying and yet so real, to her family, to the women in whose care she had played a small role – all of them a part of her indissoluble self, one that was incapable of diminution or erasure, blessed as it was to live forever through those ephemeral moments which dwelt eternally in her consciousness. Veni recalled a song her mother would sing in her low and sweet voice, as they sat around, including some of the pregnant women, garlanding flowers she and Raji had picked:

> *Alli, mallikai, tamarai, roja pu*
> Our little buds are so named
> *Ampal, ummatai, kanagamparam, kuṟiñci pu,*
> Why did our wise fathers choose for our daughters
> names of flowers, so evanescent and delicate?

Kamini, marutani, camanti, pavizhamalli
Perhaps it is because flowers are a sign
That nothing truly dies, nothing perishes!

Over many sojourns into the cave, Veni stole in parts of her life above. It seemed curious and strangely moving to her that so few of her belongings were necessary. This included the things that had held, at one point of time, great meaning to her: for instance, her *taali malai*, a sombre orange thread she had found around her neck after her wedding. For the first many months afterwards, she would touch the thread in silent veneration, marvelling at how it tied her to her man. That thread now lay in a red box and she set it aside, unwilling to wear it anymore. It was hard for him to be around her now, she understood and did not grieve for what no longer existed between them. It was time for the thread to rest. Her books, the ones she read avidly in order to teach well – those she put aside too. After all, there wasn't much more for her to know from them. Pictures, she thought. There was one of her entire family, from happy times, and she thought that that would be something worth taking along. But when she looked at the photo now, she knew every smile, every expression on each face. What was the point of carrying what was already imprinted in her memory? In the end, Veni brought with her pragmatic things: a knife, rope, candles, matches, notebook and pencils, some basic utensils, a blanket, cotton sheets and pickle, her favourite thing that Amma made using Aatha's *ooruga* recipes.

With her visits to the cave growing longer and more frequent, her family had begun to believe that Veni was spending time at the temple, where she would, in fact, often go depending on the time of the day before or after a trip to the cave, not to check in with the gods but to build a cover for her long absences. Trying to rejoin 'normal' life had failed miserably for her – a year after the attack, Veni tried to return to school and teach once more, despite her mother's pleas to stay back and quit her job. But she was resolved to show her face in public again, determined to regain a semblance of normalcy. In those early days of return to the classroom, there was always a susurrus among the children which Veni's presence would suddenly quell – the children, barely eight or nine, had heard snatches of baffling conversations in their homes among the elders and knew some great woe had befallen 'Teacher Akka' but their little hearts and minds could barely keep up. She tried hard to regain her rhythm and voice in the classroom. She had, however, completely overestimated her body and mind, as sudden attacks of anxiety and unforeseeable things – a stray word, or a sound, or the sight of a particular colour – would trigger her into breathlessness and heartache. At such moments, she would flee the classroom to the women's toilet to wash her face and catch her breath, while her poor students sat waiting, alarmed and anxious for her to come back. There were also inexplicable tremors in her body now, which made it hard for her to draw on the blackboard. Although her fractures had ostensibly healed, she would often struggle to write simple words on the board and began to avoid using it. She became prone to sudden deficits of memory, which made it hard to keep track of her lessons. Although murmurs of 'special treatment' and 'pollution' and 'sickness' echoed in the school's corners, always hushed, always invisible, the principal's unstinting support ensured that Veni did not have to face the unpleasant brunt of the nay-sayers. In fact, a few among her fellow-teachers covered for her, especially on days when Veni would disappear after taking a single class or after a particular hour. The school had shown understanding and compassion by giving her twelve months' leave, but it was not possible beyond a certain point to support her absence and three months into her unpredictable behaviour after joining, Veni found herself one day holding a letter of termination of service. It had been delivered by the principal himself, a kindly old man whose eyes had filled with tears as he handed the letter. He spoke eloquently to her on pain and misery, on the blows of life, on the solitary journey of the human spirit towards godhead, and about many things under the sun. He had also taught Veni when she was herself a child, so she heard him with respect but a cold detachment in her heart, unable to focus on the meaning of his words, unable to be moved by the old man's sorrow, unable to say very much beyond a mumble and a goodbye.

Separated from work, Veni had found the road to recovery harder than ever. She was determined, however, to not let her seemingly undetectable malaises get the better of her. She took to taking long walks, especially up to the temple and the monastery, navigating the long stretches of rocky terrain, looking out from the highest vistas to gain a sense of the world and her size in it. Her own house was turning her mad on some days, and she often rearranged furniture in it as a way to rearrange her own memories. It wasn't very successful but the physical activity was a relief and it allowed her shoulders and legs to ache and that made her feel some sensation to offset the inertia and numbness of her insomnia. Those were the days when tranquil hours would be followed suddenly by manic episodes – it was hard on her family, especially her husband, and between guilt, shame, rage, and more guilt, Veni found herself unable to break out of the labyrinths inside her mind. It was in such degradation of the spirit that she found the cave and the world inside it, and it had completely transformed her life.

Driven one day to the very edge of desperation and despair, she had nearly found an answer to her broken life in death, and it is the cave that had brought her back from the brink of self-destruction. Over the next many months, her sojourns opened her to an alternative world, one she repopulated with her own discoveries and thoughts. It was as if she had been in freefall all this while when from the skies a magic rope had fallen near her and she clung to it desperately, teaching herself to learn all over again. From the very beginning of her visits to the cave, Veni felt she had to keep it a secret – no one must know. She wasn't sure why, nor was it clear to her what her body was telling her mind or the other way round, but inside the cave, she was unmooring and remooring herself and she did not *feel* mad. As far as was possible for her to reflect upon her fragmented self, she tried to behave rationally and methodically inside the cave-world, trying to track her own actions, remembering, staying mindful and controlling the gaps in her memory afterwards. The beauties of the cave urged her to revive old, dormant patterns of thinking and being and Veni began to think of a life beyond mere survival. The psychiatrist who had treated her for trauma had once given her an exercise that she was now able to do in her own unsystematic way: try to imagine a new life, a different life, perhaps on a new planet, as a discoverer, a botanist, or a scientist of some field. The cave had given her imagination a new fillip and, in this world away from other worlds, she began to fix herself, one walk, one swim, one sleep at a time. As the hole in the centre of her being healed, it became easier to accept the possibility of the end of life too. Inside the cave Veni did not fear embracing death, a certainty one merely postponed by not thinking about it. How long these visits to the cave would have gone on, who can say, but then Chinna was attacked gruesomely and everything changed once more for Veni.

The first few days after the attack on Chinna, she and her whole family had been frantic and drifting pointlessly. He was in the intensive care unit of the hospital for days and underwent multiple surgeries. Finally, when he was moved into the general ward, the merest shell of a man emerged: not only had he no voice, the concussions to the head had left him mentally damaged. The doctors did not know when, if ever, he would regain normality. Three weeks after the attack, he was brought back home, where he sat in his room like a lump of flesh, incapable of volition or desire. Chinna's attack brought back the air of tragic lamentation in the house and a deathly pall began to suffocate everyone bit by bit. Amma took on the role of nurse and carer once again, and despite her own fragilities, Veni provided her bit, clamping down on her pounding heart each time she wiped her brother's drooling lip, or helped change a bandage, or sat with him looking out from the window staring at godonlyknewwhat. Something broke inside her after Chinna's destruction, something that had not broken earlier. Perhaps a hinge fell off somewhere but Veni thought a door had suddenly opened in the maze of her mind.

The first time she returned to the cave several days after the attack on Chinna, Veni felt oblivious to the world, yet exceptionally calm. She walked for hours inside without a sense of purpose or clarity. Something was gnawing at the base of her stomach. She went to her special places inside the cave, places she had invested with value and created memories in. She went to her beloved nook, a unique place with an overhang that shielded one from sun and rain. It wasn't much but it was near a pool, where she could bathe, and near the Garden where she could forage. She sat there for hours and thought about things her father had said, her grandmother had taught her, her mother had shown her. She thought of her brothers and her husband and Raji. She thought of her students, she recalled the two ravens that were mates for life and she remembered the way they flew in unison, dropping and soaring as one single self, united by a natural instinct that one might well call love. She thought of love, now more than ever, the love that binds animals to each other, the love that brings joy to human lives and makes us speak to each other, speak with no words, speak when the body is exhausted or the spirit is spent, love that liberates one. And she thought about what the assault on Chinna meant. That battering and the ruin of her brother was a sign: they did to Chinna what they had failed to do with her and her brother's body broke into pieces in their hands as hers did not, and they shattered his mind and cut his tongue out in a bid to silence him, as they could not with her, and this was their hate, their reprisal on her undying fire, her indomitable breath. But what they had begun, she would end. She knew then that Adhiban's final rendezvous would be with her.

The agonies of her body had receded a great deal, although ever so often, Veni's legs and groin could cramp painfully, without provocation or forewarning, and then, waves of nausea would flood her nose, eyes, and ears, making her heave, nothing coming out of her mouth, not her undigested food nor water, just the air left over from the words of abuse and humiliation she heard while four men attacked her, words that still rang through her being when she thought back to that evening by the old mill. Time, they said, would bring relief, but it didn't, and for months and years thereafter, as she forged ways to suture herself back together, Veni marshalled every skill she had learned, every ounce of her self-respect, every word and act of comfort and sharing she had received, to stand up, walk and resume where her life had stopped. But no new journey was possible without satisfying herself that the past was, indeed, settled, and every day felt to her to be a prologue to something. What it was she found it impossible to know but each day, month and year after the attack, recovery and continued failure in finding justice, Veni knew she was readying for something. Aatha used to say, young girls must be prepared for pregnancy, like young men are trained for war, but Veni felt, she *knew* in her mending bones, she was preparing for war.

What, when, how, she could not clearly see, but her body was telling her mind to organize. Her body guided her and she must hear its call, accomplish its bidding. It was time. The fading light inside the cave was incarnadine, a sight as beauteous to behold as it was terrifying, shot through with the warm, gushing blood of her body, her baby's and her younger brother's, transforming their shared agonies into a clarion call. There had been warnings of thunder and lightning this season and Veni clenched her heart for rain, sweet, all-cleansing, all-restoring rain. An old voice inside her spirit called out to her in a childlike whisper: *kuṟiñci, mullai, marutam, neital, palai*.

Veni's eyes scanned the cave's sky, engorged clouds huddling close and the sun's light moving slowly – was she imagining it? – further and further away from the cave. Her mind felt soft as the soil in which saplings take root, like an idea that grows with time, becomes larger and all-pervasive, so that in its wake, one wonders what had occupied one before. It now seemed to Veni that her going to the old mill that afternoon, the calamitous evening thereafter, and its black aftermath – these were all as unfaltering as the seasons. For after one has burned in summer's blazing fire, one readies for the lacerating rain and its purging, and then, one readies for the stupefying cold, grateful for winter's benumbing, winding slowly down into one's kernel, until spring painfully prods things all over again. Thus, it seemed to Veni that the turmoil inside her head was the beginning of a season of disquiet, the auguring of black rain that would scald the world about her, cleansing it of thick, tarry grime, the kind that sticks to everyone – man, woman, child, animal, leaf – everything. And if she could do it, could not others? And when others, then what would this world become? To the small creatures, the quiet ones, the frail ones, the fallen ones, the tired ones, the hopeless ones, could they not rise like sheets and sheets of mayflies, all of them, millions of them, several millions together, one motion, one sweep, one rise, higher and higher until they engulf the earth in a season of dark, an abyss of the skies that churns the world, transforming it irrevocably? As her mind illuminated itself, Veni felt a stirring in her being, a familiar desire whose longing she had known ages ago, and one, she thought, she had forever abjured. Like a low flame, it spread and warmed her thighs and made her remember times when her body was free from pain and discontent, those days when she could do anything, she could fly. She imagined walking upright, her head held high, her arms weighted down by achievement, and with that vision in her mind's eye, as she walked out of the cave, her heart was not heavy nor her steps reluctant.

Outside, past the edge of the great cliff, the night sky was full of constellations of stars like garlands of bright flowers and she imagined each of her brothers, Raji, her husband, every child she had helped birth, held in her arms, coddled, scolded, played with, as a star. It was all an old wives' tale, she knew, but the quiet, darkening sky glittering back at her seemed ripe for tales or memories of tales. Now and then when she thought she had seen a comet, a trail of gas far, far, far away in a universe not unlike this one, she knew that she was seeing it at a moment in time completely different from where that comet was itself at, the lag between event and perception being the sum total of its existence. And Veni wondered if our own birth and death were like that, two moments of perception, one here the next there, one now the other then, neither entire, but both singular nonetheless. And that crack – a mere flash seen from one end but many, many moons, perceived from another – is what we call life and everything that happens to us – our ecstasies and our tragedies, our plenitudes and our barrennesses – happens in that crack of time, an in-between caesura, irregular, zigzag like the bed of a river or a fracture going round a rock or a striation on tree bark inhabited by thousands and thousands of invisible living beings, that's our body – home to so many creatures – and our breath – composed of so many songs – slung between two points on a shifting orbit of perception, the distance between which comprises our whole existence.

When you saw things from this vantage, not possible without a night sky full of gleaming stars, you realized that at the heart of it all is not a forward movement in time at all, as if our future was knowable from our past, but a becoming that was independent of time, shorn of the need to arrive at clairvoyance – to know everything – and shaped instead by acceptance and open-mindedness, to remember that every pain was bearable, every degradation surmountable. Then, all events of one's life became like the broken bangles inside a child's toy kaleidoscope, the pieces with jagged edges and different colours forming and reforming infinite possibilities and combinations, yielding patterns of beauty and meaning in many permutations, all of which are renditions of one's breath and one's singularity repeated infinitely over a vast space that we sometimes call time or the ocean or the universe or sleep or a mother's lap or a grandmother's lined face.

The light had begun to fade but just for a brief moment in time, it had given her the sign she needed. The reddened sky inside the doline threw an ethereal light upon everything; even the blue-black pool shimmered in a strange glow so full of incipience. For the past two years since Veni had discovered the cave and her life had transformed, she had begun to heal from inside and out. The scars on her body had never been as potent as those in her mind, but now it was her body, lithe and strong from long hours of walking and swimming and climbing, whose tensile power she appreciated better once she learned to harness its resilience and beauty, that body was now her compass. Like an ascetic whose resolve always seems miraculous and somewhat unreal to the worldly, she marvelled at how quickly, almost in a flash, the path had shown itself to her. As she made her way out, she moved like a creature of the cave, her eyes and ears brightened by the touch of darkness, her heart beating steady to a rhythm that was one with the water and the trees and the birds. It was the rhythm of one who knows what to do, where to go next, what to say, and in that twilight hour as she walked out of the cave, ready for life, ready for death, Veni opened the strands of her thick braid. When the tendrils came free, a light wind stole between her dark tresses, and raising her arm in the manner of the great courtesans of legend, she pulled her hair to one side and unfurled all of it. As Veni made her way to her home, she knew that this was her final exit from the cave. There would be no return to the world above the next time she entered the doline.

Acknowledgements

THIS BOOK WOULD NOT HAVE BEEN POSSIBLE without the sanctuary I received at Samyukta Research Foundation, Thiruvananthapuram, where I spent the last few months of 2021 in a Covid-beset year. The love and laughter, and perceptive readings, of Jayasree, Sreedevi chechi, Sonya, Varsha, Kiran and Kuku made this book into what it is. Any fault in the book is, naturally, theirs.

I owe a debt of thanks to Vaidehi Herbert, who generously allowed me use and adaptation of her stunning translations of Sangam poetry, and my dear friend Raja for fact-checking the most scarlet of prose in the book with gentlemanly commitment.

I am eternally grateful to my family: my parents, whose love and devotion to my art knows no limit; my husband, Suddhaseel, whose acumen and sensitivity shaped the earliest versions of this book; and my in-laws, whose support and good cheer I have always counted on.

I thank my sparkling editor, Isha, for her entrepreneurial eye, which found me and was with this book through all its twists and turns; my cover designers, Bhavi and Ranajoy, and illustrator, Pradarshika, for seeing more deeply into the book's heart than I could have imagined; and Sritama, for her unfailing friendship and for taking my photo on a wintry Kolkata afternoon.

Inside my heart, Veni's voice has lived for a long time with an interlocutor, and now, they're both free.